LOOKING DOWN THE BARREL

The funeral parlor proprietress had disappeared through a small mahogany door to the left of Payne.

Now the door opened again, but this time it wasn't the woman, it was the monster in a black suit that his fleshy body had outgrown years ago, with about the meanest looking little sawed-off shotgun Payne had ever seen.

"You sonofabitch," the man said, "you lowdown sonofabitch."

"Now, Harry," the funeral parlor lady called from the small door, "if you're going to kill him, kill him outdoors."

"You sonofabitch," Harry said again, this time pushing the shotgun right in Payne's face.

"The carpet's almost brand-new," the woman said, and then, clucking and shaking her head, closed the door just as an unseen woman uttered a yelp of grief.

"You got guts," Harry said, "I gotta give you that."

"Aren't you interested in who hired him?"

"Mister, all I'm interested in is blowing your head clean off your shoulders."

Other *Leisure* books by Ed Gorman:
TROUBLE MAN
COLD BLUE MIDNIGHT
BLACK RIVER FALLS

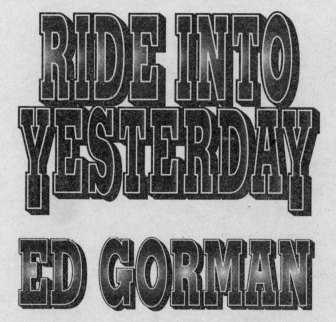

RIDE INTO YESTERDAY

ED GORMAN

LEISURE BOOKS NEW YORK CITY

*For Maxine Gill, whose friendship and loyalty
have so many times saved me.
With great appreciation and affection.*

A LEISURE BOOK®

February 1999

Published by

Dorchester Publishing Co., Inc.
276 Fifth Avenue
New York, NY 10001

ISBN 0-8439-4488-9

Chapter One

In the morning, Stephen Payne rode out there, half-afraid to go, yet knowing he had to go out to see, the barn where his younger brother had supposedly hanged himself.

In this part of the west, spring was early this year. Even though it was not yet May, silver water splashed down from the mountains and overran the creeks, tillable land was already under plow and harrow, and jackpines were full green and ripe with sweet scent.

The desk clerk back at his hotel had drawn a map for Payne, who followed it carefully, taking the wide stage road due west until he saw a dusty, pathlike trail veer east toward foothills and a farm nestled just beneath them.

A girl of perhaps six or seven, blonde braids flying, played with a golden collie in the front yard of the farm. A woman in a blue gingham dress pumped water from a well near the back door of the small white farmhouse, and out near the red barn a thickset man was harnessing a mule to a plow, talking to the animal and trying to get it to hold still. In the sweet sunny morning light, the whole scene reminded Payne of a sentimental painting.

Payne ground-tied his horse and started walking toward the back of the farm, to the man.

But he hadn't gone far before the collie, still pretty much a pup, started running in circles around Payne's feet.

'You're gonna make the man mad, Laddie!' the sweet-faced little girl said, trying to tug her puppy away, gaping up fearfully at Payne as she did so.

'He's a nice dog,' Payne said. 'When did you get him?'

'For my birthday last month.'

'You're a lucky little girl,' Payne said and smiled.

'He don't obey very good, though,' the girl said, finally diving for and tackling the dog. She was only able to hold him briefly; he spurted from her grasp and took off running, fat little backside waggling left and right, toward the barn where the man was still patiently working with the mule.

'Help you?' the woman asked.

She had stopped her business at the well and stepped up to Payne. He got the vague impression that she was putting herself between her husband and him. She wasn't a pretty woman by any means, but even in her stoutness there was a soft feminine appeal that Payne saw at once.

She wiped wide, competent hands on a soiled apron.

The girl had gone back to chasing her pup. The man had stopped his business with the mule and was watching his wife and Payne.

This close to the house, Payne could smell the morning's breakfast still on the air, bacon and eggs and bread.

'My name is Stephen Payne.'

Only after a long moment did recognition show in the woman's eyes. A frown stretched her full mouth. 'You're his brother. The boy's.'

'Yes.'

She shook her head. 'It never ends.'

Before he had a chance to ask what she meant, he saw her husband approaching. The man looked to be ten years older than his wife. He also looked strong and showed just a hint of meanness in his brown eyes. He didn't offer a hand.

'Help you?' he asked in a voice that nobody would consider friendly.

'He's Payne's brother,' his wife said.

The husband looked him over more carefully now.

What he saw was a man of thirty-five, maybe six feet tall, and about a hundred and fifty pounds, with an intelligent if not handsome face; dressed in a black flat-brimmed Stetson, a red cotton shirt, black cord trousers, and Texas boots. A lone .44 hung from Payne's right hip. The worn leather of the holster suggested that the gun had probably seen some use.

'What is it you want, Mr Payne?'

Payne shrugged. 'He was my brother. I guess I'm curious about what happened.'

'That was six months ago.'

'I just found out about it five weeks ago. I came as soon as I could.'

The husband sighed and shook his head. 'I'm Clete Winnow. This is my wife Serena.'

Payne tipped his hat.

'You two talk,' the wife said. 'I'm gonna get back to my water.'

After she had returned to the well, Clete Winnow said, 'We didn't even know he was in the barn that night.'

'That's what I hear.'

'But I don't think nobody believes us.'

'Oh?'

'They keep comin' out here.'

'For what?'

'Guess they think he buried the money somewhere on our farm.' For the first time he smiled. 'I've had men offer me a hundred dollars just to let them bring a shovel out here and start diggin'. Believe me, the way crops was last year, it's temptin'.'

'I didn't know the money wasn't found.'

'Not a trace of it anywhere,' Winnow said, 'and sixty thousand dollars is a fair amount of greenbacks.' Then he turned and looked back at the barn. 'You want to sec it?'

'I'd appreciate it.'

'Sure. Come on, I'll show you.'

'I'd appreciate it.'

'Sure can't be a very pleasant experience for you. You positive you want to see where it happened?'

Payne wasn't positive, of course. A part of him wanted to bolt, to get on his horse and ride away and just accept the fact that Art had robbed the stage and then, in apparent remorse, had hanged himself in the barn where he'd been hiding out. 'Why don't we take a look?' Payne said.

He followed Clete Winnow down to the barn, chickens brilliant white in the sunlight, following the men as they went down the sloping hill, their boots crunching through dry chicken droppings and grain that had been tossed out for the animals to eat.

The barn had two stories, a hayloft, and smelled of oil from the farm wagon Winnow had apparently been working on earlier.

Inside, in the deep shadows, the temperature seemed to drop ten degrees.

Payne raised his head and stared up at the two-by-four stretching from one side of the loft to the other. If a man wanted to hang himself, the two-by-four would be ideal: just attach the rope to the beam, set the noose around your neck and jump. With any luck, you'd be dead in very short order.

Winnow saw Payne staring at the two-by-four.

11

'That's where I found him in the morning. Hanging down from there.' Winnow made a clucking sound. When he glanced at Payne, real sorrow could be seen in his eyes. 'Twenty-three years old. Poor kid.'

Which is just what Payne had been thinking: *poor kid*.

'Like I said earlier, Payne, we didn't know he was hiding out in the loft. Sheriff Reeves reckons that after your brother stuck up the stage, he got scared and hid out in the woods south of town, then swung wide over here at nightfall and hid out in my barn.'

'No evidence it was anything except suicide?' Payne said it fast, trying to say it simply, without any flourish, but even so, he saw Winnow's eyes narrow, and a hint of the meanness return to his gaze.

'Meaning what, exactly?'

'Meaning nothing especially. Just a question.'

'You mean you think he might not have killed himself?'

'Something like this, you can't always be sure.'

'Well, I'm sure.' Winnow was angry. 'I wouldn't have no part of any killing, Payne, and that's just what you're accusing me of. If there'd been more than one man in this barn that night and your brother had put up a protest about being hanged, I sure as hell would have heard it. And I sure as hell would have got my Sharps and come down here and stopped it. But I didn't hear a thing that night, and it was a quiet night, northerly wind and not blowing fast at that.' He spat into a hay-filled horse stall where some noisy flies were busy

12

with a mound of fresh dung. 'We understand each other?' He was still angry.

'I wasn't accusing you of anything.'

'Wife's a Lutheran and so am I, pretty much. Martin Luther didn't hold with killing and neither do we.'

Payne raised his head and made a final assessment of the beam. No doubt a man could easily hang himself from there. Especially a man who really wanted to do the job—a man feeling crazy scared and guilty over a terrible mistake he'd made.

As an image of his brother dangling from the beam started to form, Payne lowered his head and said, 'Guess we may as well go back outside.'

Mrs Winnow was waiting for them, two glasses of water filling her outstretched hands.

'We're sorry about your brother, Mr Payne,' she said.

'No need to be nice to him, Serena. Sonofabitch practically accused me of killing his brother.'

'Clete, you watch that tongue of yours. Mr Payne here's probably just upset. You'd be, too, if it was your little brother.'

She handed Payne a glass of water.

He took it and swallowed. The water was good. The day was going to be brutally hot. He looked at Winnow. 'I didn't mean any offence, Mr Winnow.'

'That right?' Winnow said, still sounding belligerent.

'Clete, you behave,' his wife said.

'That's right,' Payne said, and put out his hand.

'Shake it,' Serena Winnow said. 'Clete?'

Looking like a sullen little kid, Clete clamped his thick rough hand onto Payne's.

'Thanks for your time, folks,' Payne said, already drifting back up toward the farmhouse and his horse.

'We're glad you came,' Serena Winnow said, taking the glasses back from the men. 'We just wish it could have been on a happier occasion. Isn't that right, Clete?'

Clete grunted something unintelligible. He was apparently one of those men who could hold a grudge until the day the universe started going dark.

As he threw his foot up into a stirrup, Payne said, 'I appreciate your help, folks.'

Mrs Winnow smiled. Mr Winnow sulked.

Payne nodded good-bye, eased his horse toward the trail again, and started out of the yard.

He had company for a quarter mile, the pup Laddie barking tirelessly and nipping at the horse's shank for most of the time.

Finally the dog fell away, his bark receding gradually in the hot, dusty day.

He had been following Payne ever since sunup when Payne got scrubbed up at his hotel and walked down the street for breakfast.

As Payne made his way to the Winnow farm, the man had dropped back, finding a good place to hide so that he could cover Payne's eventual return. The man had a Winchester; he was good with it.

While he waited, the man rolled and smoked four

cigarettes, the last one setting him to coughing. His father had always held that tobacco wasn't good for you. But then his father had some strange ideas about a lot of things.

He saw rolling dust, and somewhere inside that tan dust was Payne coming fast from the Winnow farm.

He set his elbow just so on the rough slope of boulder and waited for Payne to draw into range. Payne was riding too fast to notice anything off the trail.

Payne came closer, closer.

The man sighted, steadied himself again. Closer, closer, the dust thicker than ever, not exactly making it easy for him.

He fired once, twice, three times, the Winchester kicking satisfactorily with each shot.

He saw Payne's horse, apparently wounded, pitch scared to the left and saw Payne, silhouetted inside the dust, pitch to the right. The way he tumbled, there was no doubt he was hit, and hit bad.

The man waited a few minutes, considering another smoke as he did so, then raised his head and scouted the trail.

No sign of Payne whatsoever. Well, he was hurt too bad to get far.

He decided to hold the smoke till he got back to Favor where he could have some whiskey to go along with the cigarette.

He'd done a good day's work.

Chapter Two

Payne wasn't sure how long he was out, long enough anyway that the sun began riding down the afternoon sky, long enough that a buzzard was already eating his dead mount.

Payne managed to tug his .44 from his holster. He supposed the buzzard was only doing what was natural, but it still struck Payne as obscene. He put two bullets into the buzzard's head, which flew apart in three small bloody chunks.

Payne lay back down. Just firing twice had exhausted him.

He lay coated with sweat and dirt, recalling now the events that had led up to his shooting. His first thought was that maybe he had been ambushed by that angry farmer, but Payne dismissed that idea, thinking of the man's wife. She wouldn't have *let* her husband ambush anybody.

He looked around.

He was in a tangle of undergrowth, maybe fifteen feet off the trail. He forced himself to sit up. Across the trail, angling down to a wash, he saw several boulders that would be perfect for a bushwhacker to hide behind.

Pain made him dizzy again; he lay back down.

He'd been hit in his left shoulder just once, but with destructive results; the bone itself had been shattered. Blood still seeped freely. He kept trying to wave away the dirty flies on the hot afternoon, but it did no good.

He started sinking back into darkness.

Kate Cowles had sat up all night with Cassandra, well into the hot day, and sometime just after noon the kitten died in Kate's lap. She sat there in the rocking chair, on the shady side of the small shack.

Kate didn't cry much, because she had been crying most of the night anyway, ever since finding what was left of the bloody little body once the roving dog had finished with it. There were a lot of wild dogs in this area, some of them bold enough to even attack cattle.

A kitten didn't represent much of a challenge to an animal that fierce, and poor little Cassandra had surprised Kate by surviving as long as she had.

Kate took a clean white towel and laid the small tabby in the center of it. Then she carefully wrapped the towel three times around the kitty.

In the rear of the shack, Kate dug a grave, set Cassandra in the shallow hole, and covered her up with rich black earth. She made a small cross from sticks, then started crying hard again. Given everything that had happened over the past year, Cassandra had been Kate's best and only friend.

Kate went back inside and poured fresh water from a pitcher into an enamelled bowl. She took off her shirt and jeans, and washed herself thoroughly, a slight woman of twenty-four with long auburn hair and lovely brown eyes that compensated for the way her left cheek had been burned to the texture of leather. Now, self-consciously, as she'd done several times a day since she was six years old, she touched her burned cheek and dropped her eyes in shame. Even though most people did not mention the deformity, Kate was always aware that she was a freak.

Because she was due in town in two hours, she hurried into a fresh change of clothes, daubing on a fingertip of perfume behind each ear and gathering her thick hair with a blue ribbon at the back of her neck.

Then, abruptly, she was sick, the way she'd gotten more and more over the last four weeks. She ran outside to the west edge of the shack and vomited.

When she was done, she leaned against the shack, knowing she'd have to go back inside and get cleaned up all over again.

She had to look her best this afternoon, because at four p.m. she was going to tell Mr Clinton D. Todd that she was pregnant with his child.

She wondered what Clinton's wife would have to say about all this.

18

*   *   *

Payne knew that walking was foolhardy in his condition, but he didn't have much choice. He set off, weaving along the trail, falling down every once in a while, then clutching at his shoulder. Just lying there in the dusty road, maybe dying . . . certainly afraid of dying, at one point he let the filthy flies have at him, not even trying to stop them. Eventually he staggered upward and tried to walk once again.

Kate rode hard, knowing she would be late for her appointment with Clinton.

She swung her mount eastward to the narrow trail that paralleled the foothills and led to the stage road into the town of Favor. She was just giving the horse some leather when she saw a dark shape moving far down the road ahead of her.

At first she thought it was some kind of bulky animal, parched from thirst perhaps and running out of strength.

But after twenty more yards, she realized that the shape was a man. Then she saw the dead mount off the side of the trail and a buzzard with its head shot away.

Something bad had happened here, and she responded instinctively by slowing her horse and slipping her Remington from her saddle scabbard.

It was western custom to help a stranger in distress, but it was also western custom to protect yourself and your loved ones first.

She came up behind him slowly, Remington at the ready, watching the crazy way he feinted left and right, like a punch-drunk bare-knuckle fighter. Then he turned, as if hearing for the first time the hooves of her horse, and fell over backward on the narrow trail.

She saw for the first time that he was wounded, and wounded badly.

The way his legs twitched, she wondered if he hadn't just died.

Chapter Three

'Drink.'

'But —'

'Don't talk. Drink.'

He drank.

She knelt next to Payne, his head on her lap. She poured cold, silvery water from a canteen into his mouth. She poured slowly, not wanting to make him sick.

As he drank, she studied his wound. Though she had no medical training, she could see how bad it looked. Some of the blood close around the wound was beginning to discolor. She wondered if poison had set in.

'How long have you been out here?' she asked.

'I'm not sure.' He wiped water from his lips. He looked at her. She was young and pretty except for the left side of her face, where she had been badly burned.

She favored the right side of her face, which told him she was embarrassed about the scar.

'Can you stand up?'

'If I'm lucky.'

'I'm going to get you on my horse.'

'You think he can carry both of us?'

She looked down at him and smiled. 'If you're lucky.'

She eased him off her lap and stood up, leaning down to take his hand and help him gently to his feet.

Melancholy purple shadows were beginning to collect in the foothills; the breeze was cool enough to dry the sweat on his face. The day was starting to fade into dusk. She was late, and worried now that Clinton would be mad at her. Lately, he was frequently mad at her.

Getting Payne up on the horse took ten minutes. Twice he almost slipped off and fell to the ground. She had to steady the horse and hold the reins while Payne climbed up.

Just when she finally got him up there, she felt her stomach flip. She turned away and retched for a short while, then steadied herself as the sensation passed.

She came back to the horse and got up on him. They started riding.

'If you get real uncomfortable, you let me know,' she said.

'I appreciate it,' the man said.

'What's your name?'

'Stephen Payne.'

'Mine's Kate Cowles. This about the right pace?'

22

She kept the horse at a trot. Payne had his arms around her waist. He was obviously being careful not to brush against her breasts.

They were on the stage road now. Town wasn't that far away.

'I'd better tell you something,' he said.

'What?'

'Can you feel that I'm leaning against you?'

'Yes.'

'Well, I'm afraid my wound's getting your shirt all bloody.'

'Guess there isn't much you can do about that, is there?'

They rode on in dusty silence, the shadows pitched deeper and darker now in the hills and woods, the song of the day birds now giving way to the cries of the night birds. The chill reminded them that this was April, after all, and not quite real summer. The day was too short and dusk was cold.

'Can I ask you something?' Payne said cautiously.

'Sure.'

'Back there when you got sick.'

She hesitated. 'Yes?'

'Are you all right? I mean, are you sick or anything?'

'No, I'm all right.'

She spurred the horse a little. She knew Payne probably wanted some kind of elaboration but that was too bad. He wasn't owed any explanations and he wasn't going to get any.

* * *

The doctor's office was a one-story adobe building on a corner a block east of Favor's main street.

A buggy and a horse were ground-tied outside the medical office, and inside, through the lace curtains, they could see a kerosene lantern flickering against the early darkness.

She helped him down.

She could feel that he was already a lot weaker than he'd been when she found him on the road.

On the way through the door, he stumbled once. An old man with a goiter on his neck got up and helped her get Payne seated.

Doctor Pelham heard the commotion and came out of his examining room.

'Bring him in here,' Pelham said.

By now, Payne was unconscious.

He awoke to the sharp scent of antiseptic and the musty smell of cigar smoke.

A short, chubby-cheeked, white-haired man was leaning over Payne's shoulder. 'You know who I am?'

'Nope,' Payne said.

'I'm Doc Pelham. Kate brought you.'

'I remember that. At least some of it. How does it look?'

'I was just about to find out. You have any idea who did it?'

'Nope.'

'Frank's coming over. He'll have a lot of questions.'

'Frank?'

'Sheriff. Frank Reeves. Nice fella.'

'If you say so.'

'You don't like lawmen?'

'I like docs better.'

The doc paused a minute in his examination and met Payne's gaze. 'You look just like him.'

'Like the sheriff?'

'Hell, no, not like the sheriff. Like that kid. Art.'

'He was my brother. You knew him?'

'A little. He broke a finger once and I set it for him.'

'Yeah?'

'He was a nice kid.'

'I appreciate you saying that.'

'I just can't figure out how the hell he ended up robbing a stagecoach.'

'I can't either.'

'Hold still.'

Doc Pelham tore away the crude bandages Kate had applied. The blood had dried on them. The pain was blinding.

'Sorry,' Doc Pelham said.

Payne nodded.

Doc Pelham set to work cleaning the wound with alcohol. It stung, but not as much as removing the dried bandages had.

'Where's the girl?'

'Don't know. She just left.'

'Did she say she was coming back?'

'Didn't say anything, but then I wouldn't expect her to.'

'Why not?'

'Just her way.'

'What's her way?'

Doc Pelham paused again and looked at Payne. He frowned. 'You're about the talkingest patient I've ever had. I think I liked you better when you were unconscious.'

Payne blushed, feeling like an eight-year-old who's just been chastised roundly by his father.

Doc Pelham went back to cleaning the wound. Every once in a while he stopped to pick up a cigar from the ashtray he kept right on the leather-covered examination table. He blew the smoke only inches over Payne's head.

Payne knew better than to say anything.

'This'll hurt,' Doc Pelham said and, with that, yanked out the bullet.

'Sonofabitch,' Payne said, 'son of a bitch.'

'Won't bother me if you cry, fella,' Doc Pelham said. 'That's sure as hell what I'd do, somebody pulled a bullet out of me. Cry like hell.'

Payne didn't cry. He didn't want to give this old goat the satisfaction.

Doc Pelham tossed the bullet into a metal receptacle, then went back to cleaning the wound.

'Her folks died in a fire,' the doc said after maybe five minutes.

Payne had been drifting off. 'Huh?'

'I said her folks died in a fire.'

'Whose folks?'

'Whose folks? Who the hell you think? Kate's. The girl who brought you in.'

'Oh. I'm sorry.'

'She tried to go back in and save them, and that's how she got the side of her face burned that way.'

'Poor kid,' Payne said.

'You're damned right. Ruined her whole life. She'd be a damned pretty woman except for the left side of her face.'

'She's pretty enough for me as is,' Payne said.

Doc Pelham stopped what he was doing again and looked down at Payne. 'Maybe you're all right after all, son, you know that?'

Then he picked up his cigar and got back to work.

Chapter Four

Kate liked the street lamps burning in the dusk, the rush of people at suppertime, the sight of diners in nice restaurant windows, the clank and clatter of the livery running in all the stock at night. Favor was a real town, not just a stage stop, and it had remained so even though the train depot had been moved thirty miles south two years ago, taking with it several businesses and hundreds of free-spending tourists a year.

There was even a real business section – five stout two-story redbrick buildings built side by side.

She stopped in the middle of the street to pet a dog, a black and white spaniel happy for the attention. Then Kate looked up at the second floor of the center building. There was a lamp burning, and she well knew whose lamp it was.

She looked down at the dog, young and sweet and full of frisky dog life, was reminded of her cat Cassandra, of Cassandra there in her lap at the last, and felt sad all over again.

Then she thought of the child in her stomach, or the beginnings of one anyway, and gazed up at the window once more.

Gathering herself, hoping to God she wouldn't get sick, she petted the dog a final time and set off for the brick building in the center.

Once inside, she was intimidated as usual. The closed doors were imposing, the names of the lawyers and accountants rendered in gold letters, the halls smelling importantly of new mahogany trim and varnish, the stairway to the second floor seeming to reach to the skies.

A young woman like herself didn't belong in such a place, and she knew it.

She went up the stairs slowly, then stood at the top of the stairs and looked at his office. It was both wonderful and terrible to love such a man, a man she had no right to, him being married and all, a man she loved nonetheless.

She took three steps toward his door, but paused when she heard voices coming from behind the door. She looked around, saw nobody in the hall, and decided to sneak up a few steps toward the door.

'What the hell's he doing here, anyway?' a male voice said.

'Snooping, that's what he's doing,' another voice said.

'And snooping is just exactly what we can't afford.'

29

The last speaker was Clinton Todd himself. She couldn't help herself; just hearing his voice thrilled her.

Then from behind her, a man's voice said, 'Help you, miss?'

An old Indian with a broom stood at the head of the stairs.

Before she could respond, she heard footsteps inside Clinton's office, moving quickly toward the door. Then Clinton stood there, tall, handsome, curly dark hair swept back magnificently, looking thoroughly citified in a dark vest and trousers and a white shirt and cravat. But there was no friendliness in his dark eyes, only anger. 'How long have you been out here?'

'I just got here.'

He turned back to his office and said, 'A late client has shown up, gentlemen, maybe we'd better continue our meeting some other time.'

Chairs scraped backward. Male feet moved toward the office door.

Mayor McCarthy and Sheriff Reeves soon appeared in the doorway. They looked just as angry as Clinton, glaring at her as they passed her and moved down the steps, the old Indian man with the broom standing nervously aside to let them by.

She wondered why the mayor and the sheriff would meet in Clinton's office. He must be a lot more important than she'd realized.

Clinton said, 'Get in here.' Not, *Would you like to come in here?* Not, *Would you please come in here.* But, *Get in here.* The way someone would say it to a child who'd been bad. She felt embarrassed in front of the old man. He was embarrassed, too – she could see that in his glance – and he walked quickly down the stairs.

She went into Clinton's office.

If there was a more splendid place in the state, she had not seen it. This was where she'd first met Clinton, hiring him to do some legal work on the deed to the property she had inherited. He looked splendid amid all the massive mahogany office furnishings, the sentry-like rows of filing cabinets, and the smartly dressed secretaries who looked every bit as enchanted with him as Kate was. She had sentimental memories of this place and she wanted to enjoy them for a moment or two, but Clinton's mood made this impossible.

'You're four hours late.' It was an accusation.

'I'm sorry.'

'That's all you've got to say?'

'I was helping somebody. He was – '

She was going to explain about Payne and everything, but he waved her words away.

He went over to the door of his private office, where the mayor and the sheriff had just come from, and pointed for her to go inside.

She went in dutifully. She felt so many things, so many troubling things – love for Clinton, but fear of him, joy for the child she carried inside, but a terrible dread for that child's future.

She took a seat across from Clinton, on the other

side of his desk, as if she were just a client of his and nothing more.

He closed the door, came around, and sat down, with his elbows up on the desk. Despite his mood, she didn't think she'd ever seen him look so handsome.

'I'm sorry I was so angry,' he said.

'I would have been angry, too, Clinton.'

'I just – wanted to see you as soon as possible.'

'Me too, Clinton. I've been waiting all week for this day.' She hesitated and said, 'Cassandra died.'

'Who?'

'My cat.'

'Oh.'

'A wild dog got her. Poor little kitty.'

'That's too bad.'

She smiled sadly. 'But I guess you don't much like cats anyway, do you?'

'Can we change the subject, Kate?'

She stared at him, trying to fathom his mood. Hadn't he just said that he'd wanted to see her as soon as possible? Then why did he still seem so gruff and angry?

'Something's wrong, isn't it?'

'Yes, Kate, something's wrong.'

She was going to have to put off telling him about the baby for at least a few minutes. 'Tell me.'

'You know about my father.'

'Yes, I know about your father. Everybody does.'

'He's the most important man in this state. And one of the most respectable.'

She nodded, wondering why he was talking about this.

'I can't see you anymore.'

'What?'

'I can't see you anymore. I can't afford to involve my family in a potential scandal.'

'But Clinton, you and I —'

'Things like this happen, Kate, our time together, I mean. But then the people come to their senses and —' He shook his head. 'You're a fine woman, Kate. You'll find a good man and have a nice family, and everything will be just the way it's supposed to be.'

She was still in shock. 'You're not going to see me anymore?'

'It hasn't been an easy decision for me to make, Kate.'

'But you said you loved me.'

For the first time, he looked uncomfortable. He eyed the door with desperation. 'There's no point in us having a scene, Kate. This is just the way things have to be. I want to be with my wife and children now. Be a happily married man again.'

'But —'

She started to tell him about the baby inside her, his baby, but right now she couldn't get the words out.

She just sat there and started to sob, right in front of him, not wanting to at all, but unable to stop herself. She sat there and foolishly sobbed.

* * *

'You sure you can make it?'

'I'm sure.'

Doc Pelham smiled. 'You really do look like him. Like Art.'

Payne smiled, thinking of his kid brother. 'He wrote me a couple of times about coming out here to visit him. Said he really liked it here.'

'Why didn't you?'

Payne shrugged. The movement hurt his shoulder. 'I was busy at the time.'

He noticed that the doc was staring at his .44 and holster. 'They look like they've seen some use.'

'A little, maybe.'

'I get the feeling you might have come back here to cause some trouble, Mr Payne.'

'I just came here to find out what happened.'

'You don't believe the official story?'

'No, I don't.'

The doctor looked at him and nodded. 'Neither do I.'

Payne pushed away from the examination table. 'I'm glad to hear you say that.'

Payne's first steps were more wobbly than he'd expected.

'You're making the same mistake a lot of them do.'

'What's that?'

'Thinking that just because I patched you up, you'll be all right to walk around.'

'I just want to walk over to my hotel.'

'You need a good night's sleep and a few days of relative peace and quiet.'

Payne dug in his pocket. 'Thanks for your good work, Doc. What do I owe you?'

The doctor went to make out a bill and get some pills he wanted Payne to take.

After she finished crying, Kate allowed Todd to help her to the door, down the stairs, and out into the night, where he said good night to her in that brand-new uncaring voice of his. He said he had other work to do and that he had to go back up there and get at it. (The way any good family man trying to provide for his loved ones would.)

He went back inside the brick building and up the interior stairs. She counted every step he took. She heard his door close quietly.

She stood on the boardwalk, the night kissed with the glow of lamplight. She smelled the lilacs and the apple blossoms of this fitful new spring. At her feet, there were sunny yellow flowers blooming like miniature suns.

Abruptly, she started crying again, sobbing and standing right there on the boardwalk for all passersby to see.

Behind her, she heard the front door of the building open; a hand took her elbow gently, and somebody tugged her inside.

The old Indian, dressed in a soiled tan cotton shirt

and baggy jeans, closed the door behind her. 'Don't let 'em see you like that.'

'I know.' She swiped at her tears with the back of her hand and shook her head. 'I'm making a fool of myself.'

He pointed to a chair halfway down the hall. He had a small box of oily-smelling cleaning compound sitting on it. 'Sit down for a bit.'

She followed him over to the chair. He took the box off it and she sat down.

From his back pocket, the Indian took a chew. He tore off a piece with stained teeth and immediately set his jaws to working.

'I seen you come in here before.'

'You have?' she said, not quite sure how he meant that. Seen her on business, when she'd first started coming here or seen her. . . .

'You don't want him.'

So he was talking about her relationship with Clinton. 'I don't?'

The old Indian shook a weathered and jowly face. He took out a turnip watch from his pocket and pointed to it. 'You wait here.'

She was going to ask why, but he was already gone. He went down to the front end of the hall, got up on tiptoes, and blew out the lamp that lit the hall. The hall was now in darkness except for the street lamps outside.

'What're you doing?' she said.

'Quiet,' he said.

He walked back to her.

They remained in darkness and silence for five minutes.

Suddenly the front door opened up. Silhouetted in the soft streetlight was a young woman with a big picture hat, an organdy dress, and an important bustle.

She came in and said aloud to herself, 'Damn. What happened to the light?'

Then she walked over to the staircase and put her white-gloved hands to her beautiful face and called, 'Clinton! Clinton!'

Almost at once, Kate could hear footsteps on the floor above. Running.

A second-floor door was thrown open. Footsteps came quickly down the stairs.

'Clinton!' the woman cried as the tall, handsome lawyer took her in his arms there in the lobby, holding her closely.

'Oh, not here, Clinton,' the woman said. 'I'm still afraid of your wife finding out about us. After all, she's one of my best friends.'

'I don't know what the hell happened to the light,' Clinton said. 'That goddamn Indian who works here isn't worth a plugged nickel.'

'I don't know about you, Clinton, but I'd like to go upstairs.'

'Of course, darling, of course,' he said, all courtly again.

And so he led her upstairs, her bustle rustling, her perfume sweet on the air.

They were upstairs, and inside, the door long closed, well into whatever they were doing before Kate spoke.

'He lied to me.'

'He lies to all women.'

'He said he wanted to be a good family man again.'

'He was done with you. That's why he said that.'

'I feel so foolish.'

'You have a lot of company.'

'He does this all the time?'

'All the time.'

'The cad.'

'I wouldn't care if you used a stronger word.'

'How come you told me this?'

'So you won't feel that you lost anything.'

'I guess I should say thanks.'

'No thanks necessary.'

'You know a lot about him, then?'

'A lot. I've worked here for ten years.'

'Do you think he'll ever be faithful to his wife?'

'Maybe when he's old and nobody else will have him.'

'You haven't told me your name.'

'Charlie.'

'Charlie?'

'I'm a Cherokee, but the priests raised me.'

'Oh.' She had wondered why his English was so good.

'I've got to get back to work now.'

So much had happened in the past two hours. She

wasn't sure what to think about anything. She just kept trying not to think about the baby inside her.

He walked her to the front door. 'You'll be all right in a little while. Two or three months.'

'You make it sound like getting over chicken pox.'

He smiled. 'You have better memories of chicken pox.' With that, he gave her a little push on the small of the back, out onto the boardwalk.

Apparently he hadn't been kidding about getting back to work.

She decided to walk down to Doc Pelham's to see how Payne was doing. She had to keep herself moving, occupied, otherwise she would get overwhelmed by it all.

He had been kneeling in the alley for nearly two hours now. His knees were sore. His coat was too thin and he was getting cold. He was also hungry. As soon as he killed Payne, he was going to get himself a good steak dinner.

He raised his eyes once again and looked at the doctor's office. Payne would be coming out of that door sometime tonight, and when he did —

The door opened. Two silhouettes were framed in the sudden light, Doc Pelham and Payne.

Payne said, 'Good night, and thanks again,' to Doc Pelham, who closed the door. Then Payne stepped onto the boardwalk and began walking.

He sighted along his rifle. Last time the rolling dust

had thwarted his aim. This time Payne wasn't going to be so lucky.

He sighted along his rifle and let go three shots.

Across the street, he saw Payne fall to the ground.

Chapter Five

Kate heard the gunshots just as she was turning the corner leading to Doc Pelham's office.

Over the past five years, Favor had become a reasonably civilized place. A person never heard gunfire except for the occasional summer celebration, Fourth of July Day, when cowboys and drifters got out of hand and had to be carted away to sleep off their drinking.

These gunshots were different.

There were three of them, and Kate knew by the quick repetition that they were gunshots with bad intent.

Just as she reached the corner, she saw Stephen Payne pitch forward on the boardwalk.

Across the street, in the alley, a man was standing up from a crouch. He had a rifle in his hand.

41

Kate, forgetting the man for the moment, started running toward Payne. How could he ever survive another gunshot?

But just as she drew within five yards of him, Payne suddenly sprang to his feet and drew his .44.

He took off running, firing at the man in the alley, who had now retreated into the shadows.

Pure anger must have overcome Payne's pain. He ran as if nothing were wrong with him at all.

Halfway down the alley, Payne started feeling weak and dizzy. For all his rage this was twice today he'd been shot at—his injuries were taking their toll.

He was afraid he was going to collapse in the alley and maybe die from exhaustion.

But somehow he kept running.

The full moon helped, casting a silver patina over the dark shapes of the narrow alleyway. Plus he could hear the man panting. The man must have been a heavy smoker.

The man reached the end of the first alley, and then sprinted across the street into the next alley.

Payne kept up with him somehow. Each time he thought of falling down and giving up, he remembered his kid brother Art. This ambusher was obviously hired to stop Payne from learning more about Art.

Payne had to keep chasing the man, and did.

In the middle of the second alley, the man suddenly turned, dropped to one knee, and snapped off two quick shots. In the darkness, there was an almost regal quality to the orange-yellow burst of flame.

Payne dove for protection behind a huge wooden barrel.

Once he hit the ground, dust gritting his teeth, a sheet of cold sweat coating his body, his shoulder radiating pain that was almost blinding; he wondered if he could ever get back up again.

Far back now, he heard somebody calling his name, 'Payne! Payne! Let me help you!'

And he realized with a curious satisfaction that the voice belonged to Kate.

But the man was running, and panting, again.

Payne had to move. Now.

He pushed his palms flat against the dusty alley and forced himself to his feet. Halfway up, blackness lapped at his vision, and he was afraid he was going to pass out.

But he got to his feet and tried to run, staggering at first but gradually getting his legs back.

The man was leading them out of town, out to the prairie surrounding Favor.

Obviously the man knew Payne was injured and couldn't go running forever.

But given the way the man's breathing sounded, neither could he.

They passed a livery, where a blacksmith leaned over his anvil and brought his hammer down with almost mythic strength on an outsize horseshoe.

If he heard the men running past his open door, he gave no sign. Biceps swelling, face sleek with sweat and glowing in the firelight, he just kept on working.

As they reached the limits of town, buildings abruptly falling away, streets and alleyways turning into stunted prairie brush and grass, Payne decided to try to get a shot at the man.

He knew he didn't have the strength for much more running.

He didn't want the man to escape again.

Payne paused, raised his .44, sighted down the barrel in the cool starlit night, and squeezed off three shots.

The man's startled cries let Payne know at once that he'd been successful.

The man's arms flung wide, and his rifle went flying away in the darkness. He started doing a kind of crazy, half-comic dance.

Then the man quit his dancing, took two steps toward Payne, and fell straight over.

Payne, panting now himself, bothered once more by the blackness lapping at his vision, staggered forward for a better look at the fallen man.

His first glimpse told Payne that the man was probably dead. Middle-aged, fleshy, and bald, he wore a soiled checkered shirt, leather vest, black jeans, and a pair of scuffed Texas boots. He had a small scar on his lantern jaw. Dark blood soaked his chest.

Payne heard Kate catching up to him, calling out.

By the time she reached him, she was out of breath and smelled warm despite the chill night.

'Is he dead?' she said.

'I haven't checked, but I think so.' He pointed to his bandaged shoulder. 'I'm afraid to bend over. Afraid I won't be able to get back up again.'

'You shouldn't have run after him that way.'

'I wanted to find out who he was and why he wanted to kill me.'

'I can tell you who he was. Briney. Ken Briney.'

'He's from Favor?'

She nodded. 'Got laid off when the train depot pulled out several years back. I don't think he's had a steady job since.'

'He ever hire out as a gunny?'

She shrugged. 'I don't know about being a gunny, but he certainly got in trouble from time to time. Nothing serious enough for prison, but he spent a few months in the local jail.'

She bent down to Briney and checked him. 'He's dead all right.'

She looked up at Payne. 'The sheriff will no doubt have some questions for you.'

'No doubt.'

'Maybe we'd better go get him. Before he comes to get you, that is. It'll look better for you.'

'Will he be in his office?'

'No, but he'll be where we can find him. Come on.'

He followed her back into town. She moved nice and slow so he could keep up. After a few feet, she suddenly crossed in back of him and fell into step on the other side. He wondered why she'd done this, then realized that this was her good side, the side without the burn, the side she wanted him to see.

Chapter Six

'He's dead, you say?'

'That's right.'

'Who killed him?'

'I did.'

'Why'd you do that?'

'He tried to kill me.'

'You can prove that?'

'I'd say that my shoulder proves that somebody tried to kill me.'

'Somebody. But not necessarily Briney.'

'You think I'd kill him for no reason?'

'Not no reason. But maybe a reason I don't know yet.'

They were in a saloon called The Lone Dog, down by the railroad yard. The place was crowded with men and whores and smoke and the tireless jubilation of a player piano.

Sheriff Reeves sat at a poker table. He hadn't looked happy when Kate came up and interrupted him. Payne had glanced idly at the lawman's hand. He had a pair of jacks and a pair of sixes. Payne wouldn't have been happy about being interrupted either.

Sheriff Reeves was a fleshy man with thinning white hair and curiously merry blue eyes. His skin had a liquor flush and his teeth could stand some work. He wore a narrow-cut brown business suit complete with a theatrical-looking silver star on his left lapel. The five other players probably felt blessed to play with a lawman. Gave them a feeling of being a special breed of fellow.

Sheriff Reeves had listened to their story patiently, occasionally pawing at a jowl.

'He's been in trouble before – Briney, I mean,' Kate said, trying to corroborate Payne's story.

'Not this kind of trouble,' Sheriff Reeves said, 'Not attempted murder kind of trouble.'

He threw his cards down on the table and said, 'Shit – excuse me, Kate I guess I'll have to go get my deputies to pick up the body.' He nodded to the players. 'I'll be back in a few minutes, fellas. You mind waiting?'

Hell, he was the sheriff. Who was going to say he minded waiting?

To Payne, he said, 'You wait here. I want to talk to you for a spell.'

Payne nodded and watched the sheriff walk away.

* * *

Payne and Kate took a table near the back. Unfortunately, their seats were near the rear door, and the outhouse was not far away.

As men walked by, swaggering a little behind their liquor, they saw Kate and grinned. When they saw the burned side of her face they would look away quickly.

Payne saw this happen two or three times. He saw the sorrow in Kate's face afterward. He wanted to say something, some kindness that didn't sound too cloying, but he was not gifted with words, especially delicate ones.

'You're not getting much rest,' Kate said when beers had been brought them, the woman serving them glaring at Kate. Saloons did not like respectable women hanging around. It distracted the men from the other women, the ones not so respectable.

He grinned and hoisted his beer schooner with his good hand. 'I'm all right now. I've got all the nutrition I need.'

'I'm serious. You should be in bed.'

'Maybe that's where I'll be in a few minutes – unless the sheriff works up a lynch mob or something.'

'He's all right, really, just —'

'Just what?'

She shook her head. 'Favor went through a bad two years there, after the railroad pulled up and left. Sheriff Reeves kind of changed then, I guess.'

'Changed how?'

'Got harder. You know, the way lawmen are supposed to be.'

'Why?'

'Well, with so many men out of work, there were a lot more robberies and a lot more violence. Favor wasn't used to that and neither was Sheriff Reeves.'

Payne sipped his beer and nodded to the front. 'Here he comes now, in fact.'

Sheriff Reeves was alone. He went over to the card table and muttered something before coming over to join Payne and Kate. He brought his beer along.

'Well, there's one thing in your favor, anyway,' Sheriff Reeves said.

'What's that?'

'He was shot in the chest, not in the back.'

'I only shot him because I had to, Sheriff.'

'How long you planning to stay?'

'Few days. Planning to collect my brother's things and then leave town.'

'And ask a lot of questions?'

Payne smiled. 'I'm a naturally curious man.'

'Well, since I'm the law in this town, I resent it when other people start doing my job. If there are questions to be asked, I want to be the one asking them.'

Payne said, 'All right, Sheriff, then here are some questions you should be asking folks. Did Art have any accomplices when he robbed that stage?'

'Not that I know of.'

'And why would he bury the money someplace?'

'Now, how the hell would I know?'

'And are you absolutely satisfied that my brother's death was a suicide and not a murder?'

'I was told you were out to the barn. You should've been able to see that for yourself.'

'I was out there all right. It'd be easy to kill a man and make it look like suicide.'

'Well, that sure isn't the way it looked to me.'

Payne was about to say more when he looked straight up into the face of his past.

The woman who brought him another beer had been beautiful once, but alcohol had given her face a puffiness and her body a fleshiness that made her look much older than she was. In her cheap red cotton dress, her dark hair caught up in some kind of fancy style, she still seemed erotic, but it was sensuousness tempered by weariness and sorrow. No matter how many griefs a man could tell her in the darkness of her bed, she'd have even more to tell him.

'Your beer, sir,' she said. The 'sir' was very sarcastic.

Kate obviously caught the tone and glanced up. Then she glanced at Payne. He and the woman were staring at each other.

The woman smiled. Payne noticed she was missing several teeth, which only added to her air of despair.

She left then, in a swirl of cheap perfume and a final sardonic glance.

Sheriff Reeves hadn't seemed to pick up on any of this. 'I don't want you asking any more questions, you understand? If you've got questions, you come to me.'

Payne wasn't flustered by the lawman's demands. 'I mean to find out what happened to Art, Sheriff.'

'You know what happened to your brother, Payne. He robbed a stage, had second thoughts, and hanged himself.'

'That's your version.'

'That's exactly what happened.' Sheriff Reeves stood up. 'I'm going back to my poker game now, and I plan to enjoy myself.'

'I'm not trying to stop you, Sheriff.'

'No, but you're trying to stir up trouble.'

Payne met the lawman's gaze. 'Maybe I'll find out a few things that'll surprise even you, Sheriff.'

'Payne, I'm sorry about your brother. From what I knew of him, he wasn't a bad kid. Not really, anyway. But you gotta leave this thing alone now. It's over, and no matter what you find out, it ain't gonna bring him back.'

Reeves nodded good-bye to Kate and left.

After the sheriff had seated himself at the poker table and was paying them no attention at all, Kate said, 'Did you notice how scared Reeves sounded?'

'I noticed.'

'He's the sheriff. What would he be scared of?'

'Something to do with Art. That's for sure.'

In the same tone of voice she asked quickly, as if they had been discussing this, 'You know her, don't you?'

'Know who?' He knew who she was talking about.

'The woman who brought over the beer you didn't order.'

'Oh. Her.'

' "Oh. Her." '

'Yeah, I know her. Or knew her is more proper. A long time ago.'

'She must have been very pretty then.'

'She was.'

'She's still pretty.'

'Yes, she is.'

'She's staring at you right now.'

'I know.'

'She's been staring at you ever since we came in here.'

'Yes, I guess she has.'

'Would you like me to leave?'

He looked over and smiled. 'No, but I would like you to walk me back to my hotel room. In case my legs aren't too steady.'

'Aren't you going to say good-bye to her?'

'Don't plan on it.'

'She's going to be awful disappointed.'

He smiled again and for a moment let his fingers touch hers. 'I'll bet she gets over it.'

He stood up. Or tried to. He hadn't been kidding about his legs being unsteady. He had to hold on to the edge of the table. Kate came around, got him by his good arm, and helped him through the batwing doors.

The woman against the bar watched them in the mirror.

The men all watched Kate, thinking it was a terrible shame such a pretty woman had to have one side of her face burned that way.

The sheriff watched Payne, his stomach queasy, knowing that even though Payne had been shot at twice, and twice nearly killed, he was the sort of man who'd go right on asking questions.

'What's her name?'

'Myra.'

'That's a pretty name.'

'I suppose it is.'

'Did you ever court her?'

'I suppose.'

'She must have really been in love with you. The way she looked at you tonight, I mean.'

'You ever going to tell me why you got so sick this afternoon?'

They walked along the boardwalk, the lamp glow soft on her pretty face, lilacs and apple blossoms sweet on air even this chill. Spring was here if not completely, at least obstinately.

'Sometime maybe I will. Tell you about why I get sick.'

'It scared me, seeing you that way.'

'I'm all right. Really.' She yawned. 'My aunt has some rooms above the laundry in town. I think I'll stay there tonight instead of riding back.'

They walked a little longer, then she said, 'Were you ever engaged to her?'

He laughed. 'You know who you sound like?'

'Who?'

'My kid sister. She's eighteen now, and every time

I see her, she's full of questions, and God forbid I ever mention a woman, because then the questions really start.'

'I'm sorry.'

'Nothing to be sorry about. It's actually kind of sweet.'

'I won't ask you any more questions about her. I promise.'

The hotel was quiet. Nobody sat on the long front porch. Not even many drunks reeled by. Warm yellow light spilled from the lobby onto the dust of the street and the green paint on the floor of the porch.

They stood in the light, saying their good-byes.

'I've had quite a day,' he said.

'So have I,' she said.

He looked at her seriously. 'I know you have, and I wish you'd tell me about it.'

'Like I said, Stephen, maybe I will sometime.'

'I appreciate all the help you've been, especially finding me out there on the road.'

Impulsively, she stood up on her tiptoes. It wasn't really a kiss, it was more like their lips just brushing, then without another word she left him, taking the steps down two at a time, and half running down the middle of the lamplit street until the shadows swallowed her at the end of the block.

Chapter Seven

In the spring, Sheriff Reeves always got hay fever, which, according to him, was second only to prostate trouble in terms of mucking up a man's life. He had survived a cruel father, two sad and violent battles with the Creek Indians down in Georgia, the Civil War, a town council that didn't believe in paying its lawmen squat, and two children who had never quite understood how hard their old man had to work to put food on the table – but none of these battles or indignities equalled either hay fever or prostate problems. None of them even came close.

He thought of all these things as he walked along the late-night boardwalk, sneezing.

Goddamn sumbitch, he said to himself after he sneezed each time. He could just hear his wife giving him holy blazes for taking the Lord's name in vain.

The thing was, when he was inside he was fine, hardly ever sneezed. But outside —

He saw the den light on the second floor. At least the long walk out to the edge of town had been worth it.

Many nights McCarthy, the banker who doubled as mayor and presided over the council meetings, sat up in his stone mansion reading novels. He seemed particularly partial to Robert Louis Stevenson. So whenever the sheriff had late business, he'd pick up a few small stones and toss them against the glowing den window. McCarthy would gape out and wave, then invite the lawman in for a late night drink – though on the first floor, not the second, because on the second the missus was asleep and you did not want to wrangle with Lenora McCarthy during the daytime, let alone the nighttime.

The mansion – not really a mansion but a damn big house with all the finest appointments shipped in from Atlanta – sat back from the street on a small sea of grass. Reeves walked to the east end of the mansion, where the den was, and picked up a handful of pebbles, which he began tossing immediately.

The first one struck the window too hard and he shuddered. Lord, he didn't want to wake Lenora up. Why, that woman could —

The den window opened at once.

McCarthy, in his wine-colored silk robe, leaned out and waved Reeves in.

The mayor closed the window; the light in the den soon went dark. Then there were just the crickets and a lonely rushing train somewhere in the darkness to the east.

McCarthy let him in the back way.

They tiptoed through the dark kitchen, which smelled of sage and oregano, and through a dark dining room that smelled of burned candlewax, then on through the dark parlor, which smelled of sweet furniture polish.

McCarthy took him to a small room off the parlor, turned on a kerosene lamp, and went *ssssh* with a finger to his lips as he closed the door in a pantomime of caution.

He got them each a glass of sherry and sat down across from Reeves in a tufted chair.

'Out kind of late tonight, Sheriff.'

'Got a problem, Gilbert.'

'Oh?'

'You know young Art's brother?'

'The one who got here yesterday?'

'One and the same.'

'What about him?'

'He's been snooping again. Just the way we said he probably would.'

There was a primness about Gilbert McCarthy that some found almost comical. Most of the time he seemed in a daze, inhabiting some other world. He was a powerful banker only by virtue of the fact that his pappy had founded and built the bank when Gilbert was still a boy.

Now he leaned forward and said, 'It was my understanding that somebody was trying to take care of him.'

'They came damn close, Payne's got a shoulder wound.'

'But he's not dead?'

'He's not dead. But Briney is. Payne killed him.'

'Well, well,' McCarthy said. He sat back in his chair and made a spindly steeple of his two forefingers and repeated, 'Well, well.'

'If he keeps snooping, Gilbert, he's bound to find out what really happened.'

'And if he finds out what really happened —' McCarthy shook his head, the lantern light glaring on his eyeglasses. This time he said, 'My, my.'

All this 'well, well' and 'my, my' stuff always drove Reeves crazy, but what could he do about it? Gilbert was one of his partners in this whole damn mess. It had all looked so easy at first —

'Guess we'll have to keep an eye on things,' McCarthy said.

'This could all come undone,' Reeves said. 'And I don't need to tell you who'd be in a whole bunch of trouble if it did.'

'Are you saying you're worried, Sheriff?'

Am I saying I'm worried? Reeves thought. *If I wasn't worried, Gilbert, what the hell would I be doing here?* 'Sure I'm worried.'

'If you're worried, then I'm worried.'

'Then we're both worried, Gilbert. Now what?'

'I think it's time to talk to our other partner, Sheriff.'

Reeves started to reply, but held up his finger and said, *'Sssh.'*

McCarthy raised his blue eyes and looked intently at the ceiling above. 'Oh, Lord,' he said.

'Oh, hell,' Sheriff Reeves said.

And with that, Reeves swept up his hat and coat, drained the last of his sherry, and headed out the door.

There was no mistaking the sound from above.

Lenora had been awakened and was prowling around.

Reeves managed to be out the back door just as she began descending the stairs and yelling at hapless Gilbert.

Chapter Eight

Payne lay in bed with his head and shoulders propped up against the back wall, all his clothes on, his .44 lying unholstered at his fingertips.

At first, the hotel noise kept him awake – laughter and conversation, people walking up and down the corridors, doors opening and slamming.

But finally, almost completely exhausted now from the events of this long day, he slept more soundly than he had since he was a boy.

He dreamed: he and his dog Ashes running along the old creek bank; his father and mother at Christmastime, dressed up in their cheap mail-order clothes; Art and he riding the old plowhorse Dobie into the sundappled woods on a smoky autumn afternoon; and killing his first man, the eruption of gunfire and the tart smell of gun smoke, the man's friends trying frantically to save his life by covering the chest wounds with white towels that were soon soaked red and pouring a terrible amount of whiskey down him. Payne's life had never been the same after that. It had been a drunken accident, really . . . he had no intention of ever being a gunfighter, but suddenly he was one, or at least was considered one. Some men were afraid of him, others were eager to try him, but nearly everybody saw him as being not quite human. Gunfighter. Then three years later, Art showing up with his farmboy haircut and his tattered carpetbag filled with Mom's bread, a .44 of his own strapped earnestly around his hips, saying, *Hell, brother, you gotta teach me to be a gunny, you gotta teach* —

He wasn't sure if the faint squeaking noise belonged to dream or hotel room. But his eyes opened and abruptly his hand found the shape of the .44.

'You may not know it, but you're a dead man,' Payne said to the human silhouette sliding past the door into the room.

'You don't scare me, Payne. You never did.'

At first the voice wasn't familiar, but then its echoes played in his ears again and he heard, despite the whiskey and the smoke, the way the voice used to be and he said, 'You never did have much sense.'

'Neither did you.'

'You bring any whiskey?'

'Of course.'

'You going to give me a drink?'

And then she laughed and her laugh reminded him

of the old days, their old days, and she said, 'Depends on if you're nice to me or not.'

And then she came over and leaned to him in a rush of scents – perfume and tobacco and whiskey – and gave him something that resembled a kiss. Then she was standing up again and staring down into the shadows that hid him, and saying, 'I knew you'd show up in Favor someday. I just knew you would.'

Then she went over and got the kerosene lamp turned on good and strong.

She carried a bottle of good bourbon. From the top of the bureau in the cheap little room she took two glasses that could stand some cleaning, dry-washed them on the hem of her spangled dance-hall dress, poured them each a drink, then seated herself with impressive grace on the edge of the bed. She handed his drink up to him.

'Pain,' he said, and knocked back half the drink. He wasn't joking, either. For some reason, the pain of his wound was worse than ever.

She laughed. 'At least you've got a good excuse. I just drink because I like the feeling it gives me. I feel safe when I'm drinking.'

He took some more of his drink and watched her, seeing the beauty she used to be, seeing how mean the years had been to her.

She seemed to be looking out the window at the moon, but she said, 'I've lost my looks, haven't I?'

'You still look good to me.'

'My mother was that way, rest her soul. A beauty

till she reached thirty, and then —' She looked up at him and smiled sadly. 'That's another thing about liquor. When I'm drunk, it's easy to pretend I'm still beautiful.'

'You shouldn't need alcohol to feel that way. You're a good woman, Myra.'

She laughed. 'For a dance-hall girl and a whore, I'm a good woman.'

'You always liked running yourself down.'

'Maybe I just do it before everyone else does.' She tipped the glass to her mouth and took a sip. When she put the glass back on her lap, she said, 'I got to know him a little bit. Your brother.'

'You did?'

'Not very well. And I never told him that you and I used to know each other. But he came around the saloon every once in a while.'

'You really think he robbed that stage?'

She shrugged. 'I don't know.'

'You have any idea who he hung around with?'

'From what I could tell, nobody in particular. He was too busy working.'

This was the first Payne had heard about his brother having a job. 'Working at what?'

'Helping this lawyer named Clinton Todd.'

'Helping him do what?'

'Todd owns a lot of property in this area. Art sort of became his manager. Checking everything out, making sure all the rents were paid on time, cutting down weeds and painting houses whenever that sort of thing needed doing.'

'Then he didn't get into any trouble?'

'None that I knew of.'

Payne winced again with the deep, rushing ache in his shoulder. He sat back against the wall and held his drink.

'You quit being a gunny, I heard,' she said.

'I never was a gunny. Not inside, anyway.'

'You know what I mean.'

'I was forced into six fights. Somehow, through blind luck, I won them.'

'You don't get lucky like that six times. Then it's something else.'

'Well, it isn't being a gunny, because I never was one.'

'Maybe if people weren't always drawing down on you – you know how they were, Payne – maybe it would have been different for us.'

'Maybe.'

'I thought about you for an awful long time.'

'I thought about you, too.'

She leaned over and put a long, cool hand to his cheek. 'The wound – you've got a fever.'

'I need rest.'

'Is that a hint?'

'No, just a fact.'

'I can ask around if you want me to. About Art.'

'I'd appreciate it.'

She stood up, taking her drink with her, and went to

the window. 'I've been here seven years, if you can believe it.'

'You must like it.'

'That's the odd thing – I don't especially. But it's comfortable.' She shrugged. 'Maybe I'm just getting old.'

'We're all getting old, Myra.'

She sipped more whiskey and looked out the window. There was a patina of silver frost on the rooftops below, and deep shadows in the street from the pale moonlight.

'I'll say one thing for this town, though.'

'What's that?'

'It's got real spirit.'

'How's that?'

'Nearly folded up and became a ghost town a couple of years ago.'

'When the rail depot left. I heard.'

'Wasn't just the depot. The railroad took all other kinds of businesses with it, too. We sure felt it at the saloon. Business was off for nearly two years.'

'That's when the wagon works came in?'

'Right. And the wagon works attracted some other new businesses, and in a year or so we were right back where we started.' Her pride in all this was unmistakable. 'I guess that's when I decided to stay permanently. You fight through something like that and it gives you a sense of loyalty.'

'Well, it seems like a nice enough town. I'm happy things worked out.'

She came away from the window, picked up the bottle. 'You want another one?'

'No, thanks.'

'Getting tired?'

'Very.'

She'd also brought a glittery silk shawl. She wrapped it around her shoulders now. With her hair all fancy and the bottle in her hand, she looked as if she were setting off for a late-night party.

'You might talk to Clinton Todd's wife.'

'Why's that?'

'Well, Clinton's always busy with his law practice and all. Mrs Todd sort of runs things day-to-day.'

'I'll look her up tomorrow.'

She walked to the door, then paused. 'You know what, Payne?'

'What?'

'I used to pray for you. Pray you wouldn't lose when you got in those gunfights even though a part of me hated you for leaving the way you did.'

'I appreciate the prayers, Myra. I always need them.'

She dropped her eyes and her voice. 'You know what I thought would happen tonight?'

'What?'

'I'd come up here and we'd have a few drinks and then we'd make love.'

He nodded, not knowing what to say.

'But you know what?'

'What?'

'Now I can see that it wouldn't be right. Whatever

67

we had – well, it's over and I don't have to think about you anymore. Not romantically, I mean.'

'Maybe you can find somebody else now, Myra.'

She nodded, wanting to get out of there before emotion overtook her voice. 'Stop in and I'll buy you a drink, Payne.'

He nodded.

She slipped out the door.

He leaned over, the pain considerable, and blew out the lamp.

He lay in the darkness, listening to her lonely footsteps retreating down the hotel steps. Soon enough, he was asleep again.

Chapter Nine

First thing after taking a bath, redressing his wound, and gulping down a breakfast of three eggs, fried potatoes, and four cups of coffee to bring himself wide awake, Payne strapped on his .44 and went over to the sheriff's office.

The weather was nice again, sixty degrees maybe, cloudless blue sky, blue jays perched on the pink branches of apple blossoms, women with baby buggies already out for a stroll on the boardwalk, the schoolhouse bell clanging on the fresh new morning.

The sheriff's office smelled of cigarette smoke and strong coffee.

When Payne came in, Sheriff Reeves was working through a messy stack of papers on his desk.

The lawman did not look especially happy to see Payne, especially when Payne started asking questions.

'You haven't asked me to sit down yet, Sheriff.'

'I'm not sure I'm going to.'

'What kind of lawman doesn't want to know the truth?'

'I already know the truth.'

'I don't think my brother hanged himself.'

'You got proof of that?'

'That's why I'm asking questions. For proof.'

Reeves sighed and pointed to the chair. 'Have a seat.'

'Thank you.'

'You want some coffee? But I got to warn you, it's strong stuff.'

'I like it strong.'

'Not many people like it this strong, believe me.'

Reeves got up with some difficulty, given his pot-belly and his broad backside, and went over to the stove. He took a pot holder and wrapped it around the handle of the nickel-plated coffeepot.

'Watch it, it's hot,' Reeves said, handing Payne his cup.

Payne blew on it, sipped some. 'Strong.'

'Told you.'

And with that, Reeves hoisted his cup in a kind of toast. 'The mayor always wants us to greet visitors to Favor, so here's to you, Payne.'

' 'preciate it.'

'But you're wrong about your brother. He hanged himself. No doubt about it.'

'He wasn't the kind to rob a stage.'

'When was the last time you saw him before he robbed that stage?'

'A while.'

'How long's a while?'

'Six years, I guess.'

'Fellow can change a hell of a lot in six years.'

'Not Art. Not change that much, anyway.'

Reeves shook his fleshy face and frowned. 'So what do you think happened?'

'I'm just asking questions. I don't have all the answers yet.'

'You remember our conversation last night?'

'The one about how you don't want me asking questions?'

'Exactly. It still goes, Payne.'

'Tell me about the man who tried to kill me.'

'His name's Briney.'

'That doesn't tell me a whole hell of a lot.'

'Just what is it you'd like to know?'

'Who hired him to kill me?'

'What makes you think somebody hired him?'

'He didn't know me. He had no reason of his own to kill me.'

'Well, if somebody did hire him, I sure don't know who that was.'

'What happens with Briney?'

'What happens with most dead folks? They get themselves buried.'

'He over at the funeral parlor?'

'I'd be surprised if you found him at the saloon.'

71

Payne finished his coffee – Reeves sure hadn't been exaggerating about how strong it was – and set the cup on the lawman's desk. 'Appreciate the coffee.'

'You got plans today?'

'You want me to start filing my itinerary with you, Sheriff?'

'I wouldn't mind. . . .'

Payne stood up. 'You sure you don't know anything about Briney?'

'I know he had blue eyes.'

'Anything else?'

'I know he had black hair.'

Payne sighed. 'You don't seem very concerned that somebody tried to kill one of your visitors. I'll bet the mayor would be real upset about that if he knew.'

'He knows.'

'How?'

'I told him.'

'Was he upset?' Payne asked.

Reeves smiled. 'Not so's you'd notice.'

Payne got his hat back on one-handed and nodded good-bye to the sheriff.

The last thing Reeves said as he left was, 'I don't want to hear you've been bothering people, Payne. That's one thing I don't want to hear at all.'

Payne nodded, and left.

Chapter Ten

The first time she threw up that morning was just after dawn.

Her aunt, a big woman in a white flannel nightgown, carrying an outsize lantern, came out to the back porch to see what was going on.

The chickens had just awakened, soon followed by the neighborhood dogs. Somewhere nearby a cow mooed, kept inside the city limits for milking.

Soon infants would start bawling, and then adults would roll warm from bed, stuffing legs into pants and feet into boots.

'You all right, girl?' Aunt Thea asked.

Kate kept vomiting over the porch railing and waving her aunt inside. It was bad enough to be sick; it was worse to have her aunt, her *quite respectable* aunt, close by and watching.

'Here,' her aunt said, and rushed to Kate's side. 'You let me help.'

Which is just what she did, or thought she was doing anyway, holding Kate's beautiful hair back so it wouldn't get in the way of her vomiting.

'I'm really not hungry.'

'You need to replenish yourself.'

Replenish. That was just the sort of word Aunt Thea would use. Aunt Thea had gone through sixth grade, the only person on either side of the family to do so.

Sitting in Aunt Thea's sunny kitchen, the smell of new-made coffee cozy on the air, Kate 'replenished' herself, even though the very last thing she wanted to do in the entire world was eat.

She ate a quarter of a fried egg, an eighth of a piece of bread, and one prune.

'There,' she said, pushing her plate away, 'I feel much better.'

If Aunt Thea caught the note of sarcasm in Kate's voice, she didn't let on.

'The Mister' was how Aunt Thea always referred to her dead husband. He'd been a chemist and an eighth-grade graduate himself. Kate's strongest memory of him was of sitting on his bony knee and listening to him sing 'Camptown Races' off-key and pretending to be enjoying herself. He'd died slowly of the cancer, which had made her sad in an abstract way (not exactly understanding what the cancer was, being only five at the time), and even sadder about Aunt Thea who, for all her bluster and certitude, spent most of her days bursting into tears, with Kate's mother helpless to console her.

Kate sipped her coffee.

'Now —' said Aunt Thea, looking like absolute mistress of the shiny little kitchen with its icebox and fancy new tube for dishwashing, 'now I want you to tell me the truth.'

'The truth?'

'About being sick.'

'I guess I've had a touch of something lately.'

'The Mister always said to watch a person's eyes.'

'A person's eyes?'

'When a person is telling a lie, you can tell just by looking into his eyes.'

'Am I telling a lie, Aunt Thea?'

'Yes, my dear, you are.'

'I don't mean to.'

'I reckon you're afraid.'

'I am.'

'And I reckon you're ashamed.'

'I am.'

'And I reckon that right now you'd like to die.'

'I don't know if I'd go that far, Aunt Thea. I mean, the more I think about him, the less I think he's worth dying over.'

'You're going to have to do a lot of praying, my dear.'

'I know, Aunt Thea.'

'And a lot of apologizing to the Man upstairs.'

'I know, Aunt Thea.'

'And a lot of clutching your breast and pulling your hair and wailing for Him to forgive you.' She was getting pretty wild-eyed, Aunt Thea was, but then she stopped herself, looking faintly embarrassed, and said, 'Don't forget what you are, my dear.'

'A Cowles?'

'Well, of course you're a Cowles, but you're also a Lutheran.'

'Oh. Yes.'

'And as a Lutheran you're very familiar with the wages of sin.'

'I am.'

'And as a Lutheran —'

Kate put up her hand.

'Why did you interrupt me, my dear?' Aunt Thea said with no little aggravation.

'Because,' Kate said, jumping up from the chair, 'I have to run outside and throw up again.'

Chapter Eleven

Payne stood on the sidewalk, watching the slender woman working with the rake, preparing her rolling lawn for spring. Squirrels watched her, too, and a neighborhood spaniel with a sweet lonely face. A fidgety rabbit sat just on the line of her grass as if afraid to officially cross over.

The woman was working so hard that Payne hated to interrupt her, but finally he went up to her and said to the long sloping line of her bent-over back, 'Excuse me, ma'am, may I speak to you a minute?'

At first she didn't seem to hear him. She worked her rake, dry autumn leaves crackling beneath the force of the teeth, but then she stood straight up and turned around to face him.

She had one of those long, regal, not quite beautiful faces that Payne always associated with rich women. But there was nothing haughty about her; indeed, her dark eyes held a quiet sorrow so acute he was almost afraid to speak to her, as if he might be imposing. She had a small, soft voice, that of a shy young girl, though the streaks of grey in her short dark hair belied the girlish air.

'May I help you?'

'My name's Payne.'

The recognition was immediate in those sad dark eyes. 'You're Art's brother.'

'Yes, I am.'

'My God.' A smile touched her mouth. The smile made her pretty. 'Now that I look, I see the resemblance.'

'You're flattering me. Art was the good-looking one in the family.'

'But the eyes and the jaw. Those are pure Art.'

He glanced around the yard. At one end of the lawn stood a Victorian house that seemed to be only a few years old, a massive home of three stories, with cupolas and a widow's walk and fancy cresting along the roof line. The fresh white paint was brilliant in the sunlight.

'Art liked it, too,' she said, watching the way Payne studied the house.

'I imagine.'

'He made a study of architecture, you know.'

'No,' Payne said, 'I guess I didn't.'

There were so many things he hadn't known about the man his brother had become. Almost nothing; they hadn't been together since Art was a teenager.

'I understand he worked for you.'

She smiled again. The second smile was even nicer, showing charity and gentleness.

'Don't make him sound like my employee, Mr Payne, because he wasn't that at all. He was my guide.'

'Guide?'

'Do you have any idea how much your brother knew about nature or Indian tribes or railroads?'

'No, I guess not.'

She leaned on the rake handle, big strong hands tight on the rounded wood. 'Well, until your brother came along, I spent my days closed up in the house. Our boys are all old enough for school and my husband works all the time, even at night. Oh, I kept busy enough, with church and social groups, but I didn't have any fun. Art changed all that.'

Even with streaks of grey in her hair, she sounded positively girlish now that she was talking about Art.

'He helped manage my husband's property, yes, but he also taught me to appreciate everything I had around me.'

She pointed to a large, knobby oak on the east edge of her property. 'He showed me how to "read" a tree, how to tell how old it was, and what kind of climate changes it had survived.' She giggled and pointed to a squirrel. 'And he taught me that as cute as squirrels are, they're really just rats.' She made a face that was cute to see, and laughed again. 'That's one thing I wish he hadn't taught me.'

'Do you think he held up the stage?'

She looked as if he'd just stepped hard on her instep.

'We were talking about trees, Mr Payne, and animals. How did we get to holdups?'

'You sound as if you knew him pretty well. What do you think?'

She glanced away. Gone was the cute frown, the playful glimpses. The old grave darkness was in the eyes once more. 'I don't want to think of Art that way.'

'What way?'

'How he was toward the end.'

'He'd changed?'

'Very much.'

'Do you know why?'

'Not really.'

'Could you guess?'

She leaned a little harder on her rake and looked straight at him. 'There was one thing about your brother.'

'What's that?'

'If you asked him too many questions about himself, he got angry.'

'So you didn't ask him why he'd changed?'

'I was afraid to.'

'Could you tell me about the change?'

She sighed. 'What I first noticed was the drinking. He started coming to work with liquor on his breath.'

'I see.'

'And then arguing with some of my husband's workers. Art even got into a few fistfights, which really wasn't like him.'

'How long was this before the stage holdup?'

'Two, perhaps three months.'

'Anything else?'

For the first time, she dropped her gaze. 'The church bell tower.'

'The bell tower?'

She nodded, looking reluctant to speak.

'Please, he was my brother. I'd really like to know.'

'The tower is very tall. You can see it from here.'

And so he could. He followed her pointing finger to a long, needlelike protrusion against the blue sky. The tower looked to be half a mile or so away.

'I was coming back from some errands in the buggy just at dusk and I happened to look up at the tower, and there was Art. I – I had the impression immediately that he was going to take his own life. I stopped the buggy and ran up the steps to the tower and grabbed him just in time. He admitted to me that that's why he'd gone up there, to jump.'

'Did he say why he wanted to jump?'

'No. He wasn't making much sense. He'd been drinking quite a bit and he was mostly muttering. And – well, even when your brother was drunk, he kept a lot of secrets.'

'How was he after that?'

'Sometimes good, sometimes not. He seemed to drink every day, and he was no longer very friendly to me and still argued a lot with my husband's men.'

'What about your husband?'

He noticed another, subtle shift in her eyes.

'My husband?' Her voice was tight now, cautious.

'How did he and Art get along?'

'Not all that well, actually.'

'Oh?'

'He didn't think that Art behaved properly.'

'Meaning what, exactly?'

She leaned forward and touched his arm. The gesture was somehow intimate. 'Clinton, my husband, didn't think that Art paid him the proper respect. Clinton is used to people who stumble over themselves when he walks into a room.'

'He's a powerful man?'

'Very powerful. He owns a great deal of this town.'

'I see.'

'He tried to fire Art, but I wouldn't let him. . . .'

She seemed about to say more, but just then a man, a tall, trim, fine-looking man in a dark Edwardian-cut suit, came bursting through the front door of the big Victorian house, striding across the lawn.

'Is that Clinton?'

'That's Clinton.'

'He looks mad.'

She smiled again. 'He usually is.'

'What the hell's going on here?' Clinton Todd called across the lawn, not breaking stride. His face was almost ridiculously handsome, and his six-foot-two body looked as formidable as a boxer's. He was the sort of man who proved quickly and conclusively that life wasn't fair, because in addition to his looks and his might and his proud preening arrogance, he had money and power.

'I'm talking to somebody. That's what's going on here.' The woman's voice paid her husband no deference whatsoever.

Todd's eyes scanned Payne. He said, 'I told you, I'd do all the hiring around here.' He addressed Payne, 'Now, just what kind of job are you looking for?'

'Something with very little work and very good pay,' Payne said.

'Are you trying to be funny?'

'He's Art's brother, Clinton,' Mrs Todd said.

He stopped blustering then, took a more careful look at Payne, then said, 'Well, I'll be damned. You're Art's brother.'

'I am.'

The rage was back in his voice. 'Our sheriff tells me that you've been going around asking questions.'

Payne looked at the woman and then back at Todd. 'I have.'

'Well, I won't answer any of your questions, and neither will my wife.'

'I already have, Clinton. Mr Payne and I have been having a very nice chat, in fact.'

'You go up to the house, Mary Jane. I'll talk to Payne, here.'

She was about to say more, but her husband's gaze turned vicious. She seemed to shrink under his scrutiny. She glanced at Payne, looking faintly embarrassed. 'Good day, Mr Payne,' she said, her voice softer than ever.

'Good day,' Payne said.

The men watched her retreat up the sloping lawn, dragging her rake behind her. She didn't look back, not once.

'Now,' Todd said, turning his attention back to Payne, 'I want you to get the hell off my property and I don't ever want to see you here again. If I do, I'll throttle the hell out of you, shoulder wound or no shoulder wound.'

Payne didn't hesitate. 'Do you think Art really stuck up that stage?'

'You heard what I said, Payne. I want you off my property.'

'I understand you didn't like my brother much, Mr Todd.'

Payne saw the bully in the man then, anger coloring his cheeks, filling his eyes. Todd started to swing a roundhouse right that would have knocked Payne flat if he hadn't seen it coming and dodged it.

But Payne had a little surprise for Todd.

Before the bigger man had even completed his punch, Payne had tugged his .44 from its holster and put the barrel of the gun dead against Todd's forehead.

'Understand me, Todd. I don't believe for a minute that my brother hanged himself. I think somebody in this town did it for him and then made it look like a suicide so there wouldn't be any questions. And you know something, Todd? I'm half hoping you're involved, because if you are, I'm going to kill you in a way that people will be talking about for years.'

Then, to emphasize his point, Payne slammed the

barrel of the gun hard against the side of Todd's pretty nose.

Blood bloomed immediately and began running down into Todd's mouth.

'Do we understand each other, Mr Todd?'

'You goddamn saddle tramp. You —'

Todd had just started to bluster again, when Payne brought his pistol down across the man's jaw.

Todd's eyes rolled back, then he sank to one knee.

Payne kicked the man hard in the chest, and this time Todd went over backward.

Payne went over and stood above him.

'The next time you insult me, Todd, you'd better be prepared to back it up. Do you understand me?'

Todd, holding a hand over his bloody nose, started to swear again.

Payne took the toe of his boot and kicked Todd hard in the ribs, not hard enough to break anything, just hard enough to hurt for a long time.

Payne looked up and saw Mrs Todd running out toward him.

'Please, Mr Payne!' she called. 'Please don't hurt him anymore.'

Payne dropped his gun back in his holster and turned back toward the street.

He was gone by the time Mrs Todd had dropped to her knees to examine her husband's injuries.

Chapter Twelve

Outside the funeral home, Payne saw a farm wagon covered with dried mud, and a black buggy as worn as the aged dun pulling it. He assumed these rigs meant the Brineys were inside.

Three steps over the threshold of the large two-storey grey house, he was chanted at by a short, plump woman. 'You're a Briney?' She whispered as loudly as many people shouted.

'No, paying my respects.'

His response must not have sounded honest. She began looking him over. He returned the favor, putting her age at late forties, and her position as proprietor of the funeral parlor. She had a brown left eye that traveled and a brown eye that accused.

'The family's inside. May I give them your name?'

He thought a moment. 'Sullivan.'

'All right, Mr Sullivan, if you'll just wait here.'

While he waited for somebody to return, he surveyed the part of the house he could see from the vestibule. There were two somewhat grotesque religious paintings. The rest of the place reminded him of a whorehouse he'd once seen in Texas, a place too splendiferous by half, with flocked wallpaper, small wood-framed mirrors hanging everywhere (apparently, mourners were a vain lot), and a lot of cheap prim furnishings, including what appeared to be the world's most uncomfortable sofa.

The funeral parlor proprietress had disappeared through a small mahogany door to the left of Payne.

Now the door opened again, but this time it wasn't the woman, it was a monster in a black suit that his fleshy body had outgrown years ago, with about the meanest-looking little sawed-off shotgun Payne had ever seen.

'You sonofabitch,' the man said, 'you low-down sonofabitch.'

'Now, Harry,' the funeral parlor lady called from the small door, 'if you're going to kill him, kill him outdoors'

'You sonofabitch,' Harry said again, this time pushing the shotgun right in Payne's face.

'The carpet's almost brand-new,' the woman said, and then clucking and shaking her head, closed the door just as an unseen woman uttered a yelp of grief.

'You got guts,' Harry said, 'I gotta give you that.'

'Aren't you interested in who hired him?'

'Mister, all I'm interested in is blowing your head

clean off your shoulders. That's all my brothers and sisters are interested in, too.'

The yelp came again.

'And my ma,' Harry said.

Payne stared right at him. Harry was probably in his mid-twenties. He talked kind of slow. He also looked kind of slow, his baby blue eyes never quite seeming to comprehend what was being said. He looked sort of sweet in a sad, stupid kind of way, and Payne felt sorry for him, and his whole sad, stupid family.

'Harry.'

'What?'

'I'm sorry I had to kill your brother.'

'I'll bet.'

'He didn't leave me a hell of a lot of choice, Harry. He tried to kill me twice.'

'That's what you say.'

'That's the truth. And I want to find out who hired him. That's who we should both be looking for.'

'Who hired him? Whaddya mean?'

'Harry —'

'What?'

'That shotgun scares me.'

'So?'

'So how about taking it from my face?'

Harry hit him then. He took a fist the size of a saddle and drove it straight into Payne's midsection.

Payne sank to his knees.

Harry raised his knee, cracked it against Payne's jaw, and slammed Payne back against the wall.

Payne fell facedown on the funeral parlor's new tan carpeting.

Harry put his foot on the back of Payne's neck. And then put a lot of his considerable weight on it.

'You killed my brother.'

'Only because I had to.'

'Everybody loved my brother.'

And with that, Harry put some more pressure on Payne's neck and shoulder.

The mahogany door to the left opened again. Now Payne heard unabashed wailing. The funeral parlor lady stuck her head out and said, 'Harry, remember. The carpet. Please,' and then stuck her head back inside and closed the door, all with the precision of a cuckoo clock display.

Payne's wound was starting to hurt again, and he wondered vaguely if he really was going to die here in a funeral parlor.

Then the small mahogany door slammed open, sounding as if it had been torn from its hinges, and Payne saw a new face: a short, fat woman in a black dress with a black shawl and a black bonnet. She was carrying a sawed-off shotgun identical to the one Harry held.

'Let 'im up,' she snapped.

'But, Ma.'

'You heard me, Harry. Up.'

So he let Payne up.

And the minute Payne managed to struggle to his feet, Mrs Briney unloaded a roundhouse right and hit

Payne precisely on the jaw, hard enough to induce momentary stargazing.

Payne started sinking to his knees.

But she pushed him against the wall before he had a chance to hit the floor.

When his head made contact with the pine behind the flocked wallpaper, Payne went out completely, cold air and darkness rushing his senses, a small death.

'How come you done it?'

'Huh?'

'Killed my son that way.'

'Because he was trying to kill me.'

'Then he must have had a good reason,' Mrs Briney said.

'Yeah,' Harry Briney said, 'he never killed nobody without a good reason.'

For the first time since the Brineys had started questioning him, he decided to raise his head and look around. The last thing he recalled was Mrs Briney slugging him and knocking him against the wall. Then darkness and —

There were three naked men lying on long, narrow tables. Small towels covered their privates.

'Where am I?' he said, the pain from his wound returning now.

'Essie's back room,' Mrs Briney said.

'Essie?'

'Essie from the funeral parlor.'

'Oh. Then those men —'

'Deader'n hell,' Mrs Briney said.

He laid his head back down. Just where he'd always wanted to be: the embalming room. The air was tart with chemicals, and smelled unclean.

'Why'd you come here?'

'To Favor?'

'Yes,' Mrs Briney said.

'To find out who killed my brother Art.'

'Our boy didn't kill him.'

'I didn't say he did.'

'Then why'd you kill him?'

That again; they couldn't seem to understand that where Payne came from, a man had every right to kill somebody who was trying to kill him. To Payne, it seemed a perfectly logical transaction.

Payne decided to change the subject. 'What had your boy been doing the last few days?'

'Nothin' special.'

'He live at home?'

'Yup,' Mrs Briney said.

'Anybody come to visit him?'

'Maybe.'

'What the hell's that mean, "maybe"?'

' "Maybe" means exactly what you think it means. Maybe.'

'Well, maybe if I knew who hired him to kill me, maybe then we could find out who was responsible for hiring him, and who was responsible for killing my brother.'

The woman looked up at Harry, who shrugged.

'About midnight,' Mrs Briney said.

'Huh?' Payne said.

'That's when the visitor came.'

'When was this?'

'Two nights ago.'

'You get a look at the visitor?'

'Nope.'

'You hear the visitor's voice?'

'Nope.'

'Did your son tell you about having a visitor?'

'Nope.'

'Then how do you know he had a visitor?'

'Heard him get up.'

'But you're sure he had a visitor?'

'I heard 'em whisperin' out on the porch.'

'Then next day he gimme two dollars,' Harry said.

'Two dollars? How the hell come you didn't tell me about that?' his mother said.

Harry shrugged. 'I didn't want to have to split it with nobody, Ma.'

'Two dollars is a lot of money to just hand somebody,' Payne said. 'His visitor must've paid him something that night.'

Mrs Briney nodded her head.

'And you know what he got paid to do, don't you, Mrs Briney?'

'Uh-uh,' she said.

Now it was real obvious to Payne where Harry got his brains.

'He got paid to kill me,' Payne said.

'I'll be damned,' Mrs Briney said. Now it was all coming together for her, 'He got paid to kill you.'

'Exactly. And that's why I wish you knew who his visitor was.' Payne sat up slowly, realizing that he was lying on the same kind of table as the corpses.

'Mrs Briney?'

'Yeah?'

'I want to go find out who hired your son.'

She looked up at Harry. He shrugged again.

'I'm sorry about your son.'

'Aw, hell, I didn't like him all that much anyway.'

'You didn't?'

'Nah. He thought he was too good for us.' She frowned. 'He was always callin' us dumb, me and his brother here.'

Boy, that was hard to imagine, Payne thought wryly, somebody calling these two dumb.

'But,' Mrs Briney said with a certain resignation, 'he was blood, so we want to see that his killer gets justice.'

'I'm not really his killer, ma'am. The man who hired him – that's his killer.'

She looked puzzled. 'Guess I still don't understand that, but I'm willin' to let you go find 'im, I guess.'

'I appreciate that,' Payne said, easing himself down off the table, 'I really do.'

Chapter Thirteen

The odd thing was, Frank Reeves had never really wanted to be sheriff. His brother Earle had come to Favor right after the war, when the place was much smaller, and taken on the job of town marshal. The pay had been fifty dollars a month. Eventually, Favor and the job grew bigger, and Earle needed some help, so he wired his brother and asked if he wanted to be deputy. Frank, who'd been having no success selling farm goods, said hell yes, sure, and left immediately for Favor.

Frank Reeves had never been one for wearing a gun, and in fact, going armed still made him nervous. A man who wore a gun was more likely to get shot by a gun, he always reasoned – somebody else's. But now, after fourteen years, Favor was his home, and he'd enjoyed his time here with a couple of notable exceptions.

And this was sure as hell one of them, Art Payne's

brother showing up and asking a lot of questions.

Now he sat with his feet up on his desk, his Stetson pulled low over his face, and a cup of coffee growing cold and perched on the slope of his belly.

He was thinking, and he wasn't liking what he was thinking at all: that Payne had survived two attempts on his life but he might not survive three.

The bell above his door jingled. The heavy footfall of boots sounded on his floor.

Reeves tilted his hat back and his head up, and looked into the sneering face of Clinton Todd, accompanied by the mayor.

'I rest a little easier knowing that our sheriff is taking a nap at ten in the morning,' Todd said, speaking in his favorite tongue, sarcasm.

'I was thinking a little bit,' Reeves said, unexcited by Todd's bullying. 'You should try it sometime.'

'Now, now,' Gilbert McCarthy said. 'Nothing's going to work out right for us if we can't get along among ourselves.'

Todd went over to the potbellied stove and poured himself a cup of coffee. He didn't ask the mayor if he wanted any.

Todd turned back to the two men and said, 'Well, he's out asking questions again this morning.'

Just then, Reeves noticed the bruises on the right side of Todd's fancy handsome head. He wondered who had had the pleasure of putting that bruise there.

'You run into a little trouble somewhere, Clinton?'

'The sonofabitch had his gun out before I knew what

happened.' Todd glared at him. 'If you were any kind of a lawman, you'd get up off your fat ass and arrest him.'

'I assume you provoked him.'

'I took a swing at him, but so what? He was on my property, asking my wife questions.'

'Your wife?' Reeves said, sitting straight up in his chair. 'She tell him anything?'

McCarthy waved his hand. 'She doesn't know anything to tell him, Reeves. Now calm down. We're the only three people who know what happened to Art Payne, and so long as we don't say anything, nobody will ever know.'

'I agree with Clinton,' Reeves said. 'I don't like the idea of him going all over town and asking questions. If he does that long enough, he may just turn something up.'

'I thought you warned him about asking questions,' Todd said. 'Why the hell don't you go after him?'

'And arrest him for what exactly, Clinton?' Reeves said. 'His brother died and he wants to know a little more about the circumstances. You can't jail a man for that. Hell, he'd hire himself Donovan as a lawyer and Donovan would get ahold of Judge Crane, and Crane would start gnawing on my ass till I set Payne free. You know that.'

'You're the *sheriff*,' Todd said, petulantly.

'Yes, Clinton, but I didn't write the Constitution,' Reeves said.

'Then what're we going to do, gentlemen?' McCarthy said.

'Nothing to do but hope he runs into a dead end,' Reeves said, 'and leaves town.'

'Exactly when the hell do you think that's going to be?' Todd said.

Reeves shrugged. 'Maybe sooner than we think. He's going to get tired of asking questions and not getting any answers.'

'You mean you're just going to sit there and do nothing?' Todd said.

'I think the sheriff is right, Clinton,' McCarthy said. 'The more we push him, the longer he's bound to stay.'

'What the hell do you know about anything?' Todd snapped at McCarthy. 'Of course you'd want to back off from a gunslinger. You're afraid of your own wife.'

'I'm telling you, Clinton,' Reeves said, 'you're borrowing trouble.' He pointed to the right side of his face. 'He messed you up a little. It isn't worth paying him back.'

Clinton Todd looked at his two companions and shook his head. 'I wish you two could hear yourselves. You're just going to let this guy walk around Favor and ask all the questions he wants, aren't you?'

The sheriff and the mayor glanced at each other.

'I guess that's right, Clinton,' Reeves said.

'Well, it may be right for you two,' Todd said, 'but it sure as hell isn't right for me.'

And with that, he snapped up his hat, slammed it down on his head, walked over to the door and jerked it open, then hurled the door shut behind him.

'What do you think he's going to do?' the mayor said.

'That's the hell of it,' the sheriff said.

'What?'

Reeves shook his head. 'I'm almost afraid to find out.'

Chapter Fourteen

Payne stood on the boardwalk for a long time, staring at the three-story white frame house with the ROOMS FOR RENT sign on one of the porch pillars.

Now, near noon, shade covered much of the house, thanks to three huge oak trees, and the good smell of baking bread came from the kitchen. On the porch railing, a small grey kitty with big green eyes and a sweet little profile sat stretching and yawning with her prim pink mouth.

A great loneliness came over Payne as he stood here and imagined his brother Art walking up the front porch steps or sitting on the porch some firefly summer night and talking with other boarders or scooping snow from the stoop with a shovel that sparkled in winter sunlight.

A life had been led here, his brother's life, for nearly four years, and Payne thought how sad it was that there seemed to be no trace of him left here, that it was now just a house of strangers.

On his way up to the front door, he stopped and scratched the kitty on the head. She purred gratefully.

The door was opened after two knocks. A woman in a faded flowered cotton dress stood there, a woman with grey hair and pleasant features and eyes hidden behind dark glasses.'

'Mrs Engstrom?'

'Yes.'

'My name is Payne.'

'My Lord!'

'Ma'am?'

'Your voice, I thought I heard Art in that voice.'

He saw then, in the way that her fingers fluttered mothlike at the screen, that she was blind. Hence the dark glasses.

She pushed the door open. 'Won't you come in?'

'Thank you.'

The house smelled even more sweetly now of baking bread. She led him into a parlor, where throw rugs, doilies, fancy Victorian lamp shades, and a massive brick fireplace lent the whole house a gentility that made Payne want to move in, just as Art had.

'Would you care for some tea?'

'No, thanks, ma'am.'

'Would you mind if I had some?'

'Not at all.'

He watched her pour from a fancy china pot into a fancy china cup.

She certainly didn't move like a blind person. She moved quickly, certainly.

She touched the cup to her mouth and then said, 'I miss him. Art, I mean.'

'So do I.'

'He was a fine young man.'

'Thank you for saying that.' He paused and glanced over at a built-in shelf filled with books. They were good, leather-bound editions. He'd always wanted to be a reader and to sit in a room like this.

'Mrs Engstrom, do you believe Art was the kind of person who would rob a stage?'

'Toward the end of his life, your brother changed a great deal.' Mrs Engstrom sounded apologetic.

'Do you know why?'

'I'm not sure. But every once in a while I'd hear him muttering to somebody on the front porch late at night.'

'Would you happen to know who that was?'

She hesitated again. 'I'm afraid I'm about to get myself in some trouble.' She sat very stiff on the edge of her seat and then took a long drink of her tea. 'Do you know a man named Clinton Todd?'

'Yes.'

'He was the man who was coming to see your brother.'

'Do you know why?'

'No.'

'But you're sure it was him?'

'When you lose your sight – which, fortunately, I

didn't do until I was well into my fifties – you develop your other senses. I've heard Clinton at enough town council meetings to recognize his voice.'

'Did you know a man named Briney?'

'The one who tried to kill you?'

'Yes. How did you know that?'

'Favor's a progressive town, Mr Payne, but still a relatively small one.' She shook her grey head. Her glasses were completely dark.

Payne said, 'Do you think I could see his room?'

'Your brother's?'

'Yes.'

'Of course.' She smiled. 'In fact, I'm impressed that you asked to. It shows that you come from good, caring people.'

'I like to think I do,' Payne said, an image of his parents coming to mind.

She came up to him and touched his sleeve. 'It takes me a little while to get up the steps, but we'll make it eventually.'

She started to lead the way out of the room, then said, 'His room is pretty much the way he left it.'

'You haven't rented it?'

She laughed. 'I know it's sentimental. But Art and I were very close – except toward the end.'

She led the way out of the room and up the stairs.

He sat on the edge of a single bed and sorted through a sack of odds and ends Art had left behind: a jack-knife, a comb, a catch for a string tie, a pair of spurs so fancy nobody but a drunken peacock of a cowboy would ever wear them.

He went to the closet and opened the door. The clothes were mostly faded, running to a few blue work-shirts and grey workpants. On the floor, he found two pairs of worn boots. He held them up and smiled at them. Art's feet had grown considerably, maybe to size thirteen.

He finished by going to the bureau and looking through the drawers. Some yellowback novels, mustache wax (though as far as Payne knew, Art had never grown a mustache), and a fancy cravat that Payne couldn't imagine his brother wearing.

Memories of Art came quickly. Art as a very young boy, later as a teenager.

Then, in the bottom of the bottom drawer, Payne found a ticket from the local livery. Payne was curious what it was for, and stuffed it in his pocket.

The loneliness was back: Art gone, his parents gone, and no woman or prospect of any in his life. He stared out the window at the sunlight dappling through the shade trees and falling on the sidewalk below. Art must have found this room peaceful and comfortable. He could imagine him lying on the bed and reading a yel-lowback.

Then he smiled, a good memory filling him with real joy: reading to Art when they'd been young and Art fascinated to the point where he'd follow Payne around and say, 'Wead to me, wead to me.'

Payne went over to the bed and touched his hand to

the pillow. 'So long, brother,' Payne said, a formal good-bye to the brother he should have stayed in much closer touch with.

Then he went back downstairs.

'I'm glad I got to meet you, Mr Payne.'

'It was nice to meet you, too, Mrs Engstrom.' He paused. 'You know, you never did answer my question.'

'I was hoping you'd forgotten.'

'So you think he really did rob that stage?'

She spoke very softly now, and sadly. 'Yes, Mr Payne . . . yes, I'm afraid he did.'

Chapter Fifteen

Payne was on his way back to his hotel when he saw Kate.

She sat on the edge of the small civic park with the looming Civil War memorial, staring at her hands folded in her lap.

He waited for a heavy, jangling farm wagon to roll past, then walked over to her, glad to be among the red and yellow flowers and the greening grass of the park.

'Morning.'

'Morning,' she said back.

She'd seen him coming, but now she kept her head down.

'Mind if I sit down?'

'If you'd like.'

'Boy, there's enthusiasm.'

She raised her face. 'Just don't say anything, all right? I mean, let's just sit here.'

'Fine.'

He tried hard not to notice that she'd been crying. He didn't want to make her any more uncomfortable than she already was.

He watched robins and jays and woodpeckers; he watched babies and old ladies with canes and old men with lumps of tobacco in their mouths; he watched buggies and horses and dogs and cats and even one little pink pig with a blue ribbon around its neck being led down the street by a young man.

Finally, she said, 'I wouldn't blame you.'

'Huh?'

'For wanting to get up and leave.'

'Who said I wanted to get up and leave?'

'Well, we aren't saying anything.'

'That doesn't mean I'm not enjoying myself,' Payne said.

'Men don't like to sit and do nothing.'

He smiled and said, 'Now whoever told you that?'

She looked at his shoulder. 'Still hurt?'

'Some.'

'You finding out anything about your brother?'

'Not as much as I'd like.' He watched an ice wagon roll by, water trickling from the back. 'You know a man named Clinton Todd?'

'You trying to be funny?'

'No, why?' Payne said.

'You mean of all the men in this town, you just happened to pick his name out of the air?'

He sensed she was getting worked up again, maybe

ready to cry. 'I'm sorry if I said something wrong, Kate. But I want to find out about this Clinton Todd. He may know something about my brother's death.'

She raised her head and looked at him as if she were going to speak, but stopped herself and let her gaze fall to the ground again.

They sat in silence once more.

Across the street, a merchant in a white shirt with bright red sleeve garters and a new white apron came out to the boardwalk and started sweeping away the dust. In the store window another man in an identical white shirt and white apron and bright red sleeve garters shaped a fancy display of men's shirts.

'You mind if I talk to you?' she asked Payne.

'Only if you want to.'

'I'm probably going to shock you.'

'I've been shocked before and I seem to have survived it all right.'

'It's just that I don't have anybody else to talk to except Aunt Thea.'

'I see.'

'I don't suppose this makes much sense.'

'Not so far.'

'I really don't have anybody else to talk to.'

'Then talk to me.'

She looked away to the Civil War memorial, where an iron soldier in uniform rested wearily on his long rifle and gazed up at the heavens for guidance or rescue, Payne couldn't quite tell which.

'You know you mentioned Clinton Todd?'

'Yup,' Payne said.

'I've been seeing him.'

'I see.'

'He's married.'

'I know,' Payne said.

'I'm pregnant.'

'And the child —'

'It's his child. Clinton's.'

Now it was Payne's turn for silence. He wasn't sure what to say. 'You know what you're going to do yet?'

'Not yet.'

He put a hand on hers. 'Why don't you calm down a little?'

'You're really nice. To listen to me, I mean.'

He smiled. 'You're nice, too.'

'I'll bet Clinton's wife wouldn't say I'm nice.'

He noticed that he'd forgotten to move his hand away from hers. He thought about it a moment and decided to leave it there.

'I probably wouldn't have been so stupid if it hadn't been for the fire,' she said.

'The fire?'

'The way my face is burned.'

'I see.'

'Clinton is so handsome and all. I guess his paying attention to me – well, for the first time I felt like a normal young woman. I even forgot about how my face looks.'

'Have you told him you're pregnant?'

'Not yet.'

'You plan on it?'

'He doesn't want to see me anymore.'

'He tell you that?'

She nodded. 'Yes. Then Charlie showed me why.'

'Charlie?'

She told him about the old Indian who swept up Clinton's building and how Charlie had hid her so she could see that Clinton was already seeing another woman, and how Clinton did those things on a regular basis, sort of turning over women the way some men turn over cards in a game of blackjack.

Payne felt bad about what he said next, but he couldn't help himself. 'Would you consider doing me a favor?'

'Sure.'

'Go and talk to Charlie with me tonight.'

'To Charlie?'

'I want him to help me break into Todd's office.'

'Oh, no. No, I couldn't do that.' She sounded positively scandalized.

"It's important. Maybe if I can get into his office, I can find out what he had to do with my brother's death.'

She looked shocked again. 'Clinton wouldn't do something like that.'

'I'm afraid he would,' Payne said, thinking of how the blind woman had spoken of Todd's late-night visits to his brother.

'I just couldn't do that to Clinton.'

'Because he's been so nice to you, huh?'

109

Fortunately, she saw the humor in his remark. 'I guess I had that one coming.'

'No, it's all right. I pretty much know the kind of man Clinton is.'

He took her hand again and raised his eyes to her face. It felt good holding her hand this way, and he realized that he was hardly aware of her burned face at all now. She just looked pretty.

'I'm a foolish woman,' she said.

'That's one thing all human beings have in common,' he said.

'What's that?'

'When you come right down to it, we're all kind of foolish.'

She laughed. 'You sure have a funny way of looking at things sometimes.'

'I have to, otherwise I'd go crazy.'

'You seem too strong to go crazy.'

'Oh, no. I'm just as weak as anybody else. And I get just as confused. People lie a lot and I never know what to make of it. They say they're your friend but they're not, and they say you can trust them but you can't. So it makes you feel crazy sometimes – like you're all alone and there's nobody you can count on.'

'You can trust me.'

He stared at her. 'I hope that's true, Kate. I sure want to trust you.'

He showed her the ticket stub he found in Art's drawer.

She took it, held it up to the light, read the printing on it. 'It's from the livery.'

'Right. Why would they have tickets like this?'

She started to shake her head and said, 'Oh, wait a minute. The surrey.'

'What surrey?'

'Well, you know how expensive those new surreys are. There're only two or three in town.' She frowned comically. 'Clinton has one of them, of course. But anyway, the blacksmith at the livery decided to buy a surrey and rent it out for an hour at a time. He always gives you tickets.'

'And that's what this is?'

'Right.'

'I wonder why Art rented a surrey?'

'You could always ask the blacksmith. He's a pretty nice man, except when he's drinking.'

Payne stood up. 'So what about you? What're you going to do the rest of the day?'

'Think, I guess. Try to figure out what to do.'

'It won't be an easy decision.'

She sighed, nodded, and looked off into the distance again.

'Why don't you give me your aunt's address? I'll stop by later this afternoon.'

She stood up now, too. 'It's really been nice, seeing you.'

'Yes, it has,' he said, and leaned over and kissed her tenderly on the cheek. The one with the burn.

She gave him the address, then watched him walk

111

away, down the dusty street and into the colorful noon-day crowd.

He was a curious man, lonely and angry in his quiet way, but she sensed he was honorable and she liked him in a way she'd never quite liked a man before.

Chapter Sixteen

After the war, there were a lot of men like Cooley and Haskins. Finding nothing left for them in the south, they drifted southwest and west, only to find that they weren't suited any longer for the sort of day-labor jobs they'd had before Jefferson Davis set everything in motion. War had changed them. While they might not be exactly like the brutes who made up the Jayhawkers, or the even more brutish sorts who followed Quantrill, they were predisposed to doing jobs just on the cusp of legality. Sometimes this meant arson or modest stickups, and sometimes it meant violence. But it never meant murder, because the west had developed a real appetite for hangings.

Executions had become social events in many parts – hell, in Nevada they were hanging three men at the same time, and people were coming from as far as one hundred miles away to see them, and spending the whole day gorging on potato salad and beer to celebrate the event – so Cooley and Haskins knew better than to kill a man. They were relatively young men, and there was still the chance that they'd find gold or learn that they were heirs to a diamond fortune in Africa or that they'd save a rich man's daughter from drowning – something would turn up, they were sure of it just as most relatively young men are sure of it. They didn't want to go spoiling their chances by being the entertainment for five hundred drunken folks who liked nothing better than a good execution.

Cooley and Haskins had nothing against a life of crime, so long as it was a life of petty crime.

After leaving the sheriff's office, Clinton Todd went back to his own office and spent the rest of the morning shouting obscenities at his secretary, a pale, cowering woman he took undue pleasure in berating.

Finally, when she broke into tears, he gave up his shouting, slammed shut the door to his private office, and spent the next hour in one of his favorite pastimes, sulking.

Stephen Payne had to be dealt with, no doubt about it. Maybe Reeves didn't see it, maybe McCarthy didn't see it, but Clinton Todd saw it and by God he aimed to do something about it.

And that was when he thought of Cooley and Haskins.

A year ago, Todd had been seeing one of the young women who ran the local millinery store. She was young, and if not pretty then certainly attractive. Best of all, she was *new*. Later she'd gotten foolish about things and threatened to go see Todd's wife and tell her everything, so Todd had paid Cooley and Haskins to 'persuade' her to leave town quietly.

He got up abruptly from his desk, went into the front office, and informed his still-teary secretary that he would be back later that afternoon.

He made certain to slam the door.

His first reaction was to cover his nose with his hand. The stench was terrible, And, by the mooing, he didn't have to wonder what the two were up to.

Cooley and Haskins lived in a small log cabin that sat next to a winding silver creek. In back they usually kept a cow, which they planned to butcher when the time came.

Apparently, the time had come.

When he got around back, Todd saw the unconscious animal lying on her side. Using a long knife that resembled a machete, Cooley was gutting her. Blood and entrails gushed out. From nowhere, what seemed like hundreds of flies appeared. They made a terrible, filthy noise.

'Hey there, look who's here,' Haskins said, glancing up at Todd.

The two could have been twins. They both preferred to wear long underwear and trousers with suspenders and boots so old their toes peeked through. They bore great, ratty beards, the only difference being that Cooley's beard was red and Haskins' was black

Cooley stuck his hand deep inside the dead animal and ripped out a handful of bloody guts, which he flung in the creek.

'She's gonna taste good, you can bet on that,' Cooley said.

'Sure makes me hungry,' Todd said, knowing that his sarcasm would be lost on them. 'You suppose we could step down by the creek and talk?'

The two men looked at each other and grinned, obviously taking pleasure in making Todd uncomfortable.

Just to up the ante a little, Cooley stuffed his hand inside the cow once more, wiggled it around, and brought out another pile of entrails. These were still so fresh, they were steaming.

Todd drifted down by the creek.

Cooley and Haskins followed in a few minutes.

Haskins went over to the creek bed, dropped to his knees, and washed off his hands.

Cooley stood talking with Todd, Apparently he had no intention of washing. He held his hands out from his body a few inches, where the flies circled and circled them with noisy enthusiasm. If flies could sound grateful, these flies did.

Todd told them what he had in mind. It was simple, really. Cooley and Haskins had done such work many times, for many people.

When he was finished, all Cooley said was, 'How much?'

'How much do you want?'

They looked at each other.

'Thirty,' Haskins said.

'Forty,' Cooley said.

'Right,' Haskins said, 'Forty. Forty it is. Just so long as you understand what I want done.'

Cooley looked at Haskins and smiled. 'Oh, we understand all right.'

Twenty minutes after Todd left, Cooley and Haskins took two dusty, empty potato bags and two long sticks that resembled canes, and went down by the creek into the tall reeds where they began beating the soft, smelly mud.

It didn't take long to find a snake, but unfortunately the first little bugger got away, so Cooley and Haskins went back to pounding the mud with their sticks and soon enough another one showed up.

Cooley was actually afraid of the damned things, so Haskins had to do most of the real work. Cooley just held the potato sack open so Haskins could get the snake inside. And once it was trapped, Cooley quickly handed the sack to Haskins.

'Gonna be fun,' Cooley said.

'Gonna be real fun,' Haskins said.

The potato sack in his hand was jumping around. That little pecker was sure mad.

Gonna be real fun, it was.

Chapter Seventeen

A blacksmith, brown as an Indian, sweat rolling in plump crystal beads down his wide face and immense chest and forearms, stood pounding his hammer against a burning-red horseshoe. There was a powerful music in the clang of hammerhead to anvil.

Payne watched, fascinated as any kid.

The livery smelled of sweet hay and manure.

In the stalls, two gentle-faced horses watched the whole process, their tails switching flies, their noses twitching at odors only they could detect.

Finally, the blacksmith looked up. He didn't quit his work, but simply took notice of Payne. 'Help you?' All he wore was a doeskin vest and jeans. The vest was soaked dark with sweat.

Payne held up the ticket stub he'd found in Art's room.

'Wondering if you could tell me anything about this?'

He held the stub closer to the man's face.

'One of them tickets we use when we rent surreys,' the blacksmith said.

'That's what I was told.'

'Nothin' special about it, mister. A lot of people in Favor rented them surreys.'

'I'm thinking of one person in particular.'

'Who?'

'Art Payne.'

The blacksmith's eyes narrowed and his mouth grew tight. So did his voice. 'The sonofabitch who robbed the stage?'

'He happened to be my brother, mister. I'd appreciate it if you'd watch your mouth.'

The blacksmith shrugged, 'No offense, mister. I just don't hold with robberies.'

'Believe it or not, neither do I.'

The blacksmith's eyes softened then. 'Sorry about what happened to him, mister. Hanging himself that way. Had an uncle who did that. My old man had to cut him down personally. Never did get over it. Even when he was real old, my old man would cry about it late at night.'

'Did Art rent surreys from you?'

'Yep. Yep, he sure did.'

'Frequently?'

The blacksmith thought about this. 'Well, for a cer-

Ed Gorman

tain period there, he seemed to take one every other night or so.'

'Know how long he kept them?'

The blacksmith clanged his hammer down on the fiery horseshoe again. 'All I know is that in the morning, the surrey was parked behind the barn here, and the horse was put away.'

'So he always brought them back late?'

'Guess so.'

'You ever find anything in the surrey afterward?'

'Find anything?'

'You know, something somebody might have dropped.'

The blacksmith thought again a moment. Then he raised and brought down his hammer with impressive force. 'Can't say I ever found anything right after he used it, but from time to time I'd pick up things people would leave behind in the surreys. Odds and ends.'

'You keep 'em?'

'They're in a box over there.'

'Mind if I take a look?'

The blacksmith shrugged. 'I'll get it for you.'

He went over and redeemed a small cigar box. The lid had been torn off.

Payne sifted through the odd buttons, cigars, collar bars, and pieces of lace that had torn off hems and cuffs. He found only one thing he wanted to keep. He held it up and showed the blacksmith. 'Can I take this?'

'If you want, sure.'

'Thanks.' He dropped the object in his pocket. 'Any idea of what Art did with the surrey?'

'Nope, and it wasn't any of my business, either.' He glared at Payne. 'I'm sorry about your brother, mister – nice young kid gettin' involved in a robbery and all – but I sure as hell don't see the point of these questions.'

'I just find it odd that somebody Art's age would keep renting a surrey.'

'Well, I'm sure he was courtin' somebody.'

'You have any idea who?'

'Afraid I don't.' He raised his hammer and pointed to the loft. 'You could always ask Rupert.'

'Rupert?'

'Drunk I let sleep here 'cause he keeps the barn and the horses clean for me.'

'He up there now?'

The blacksmith grinned. 'Heard him snorin' before you came in.'

Payne used the ladder. The closer he got to the loft itself, the more he sneezed. He'd had allergies as a boy, and the infirmity had never quite left him.

Sprawled in the hay, a horse blanket covering the bottom half of his body, was a scrubby man in a torn suit and filthy white shirt that were a parody of respectability. He needed a shave at least as bad as he needed a bath.

Payne knelt next to him and shook him awake.

'Ma! Ma!' Rupert cried out, apparently waking from a terrible dream. It was odd to see a man in his fifties

121

still call out for his mother that way, but maybe even old men – in the last moments of their lives – did just that. Maybe people stayed children no matter how old they got.

Rupert sat up. His stench was terrible. 'Who're you?' he said, frightened, uncomprehending brown eyes darting about.

'Payne.'

'Payne? Any relation to Art Payne?'

'Brother.'

'Oh.'

Rupert was coming awake now. Despite the fact that he filled the air with the vapors of his drinking, the first thing he did was wiggle two grimy fingers into the watch pocket of his vest and extract a cigar butt. He lit it with a match that he scratched on the sole of his shoe, right next to the hole it bore.

He blew smoke like a railroad tycoon and said, 'You wouldn't happen to have a drink on you, would you, buster?'

'Afraid not.'

Payne heard something rustle in the straw behind Rupert's head. A plump rat the size of a kitten hunched there, red eyes glowing.

'That's a hell of a rat,' Payne said.

'I call him Mike. Sonofabitch is under the impression the two of us are pals. Can't get rid of the bastard.'

Despite himself, Payne smiled. Then he said, 'Were you ever here late at night when my brother brought the surrey back?'

'Sure wish you had a drink on you.'

'How about my brother?'

'Guess I was. Few times, anyway.'

'You ever see anybody with him?'

'Nope, not that I can remember.'

'He ever say anything to you about his surrey rides?'

Rupert grinned with stumpy little teeth. 'No, but I heard him whistling.'

'Whistling?'

'You know, the way a fella does when he's happy. Very happy.'

'How many times you hear him do that?'

'Most nights I was here.'

'But he never mentioned who he was seeing?'

'Not by name. But a couple of nights I got close to him, and he sure smelled good, let me tell you.'

'Perfume?'

'Expensive perfume.' Then he snapped his fingers. 'Oh, wait. I nearly forgot.'

'Forgot what?'

'I guess I did see somebody with him here one night. The only time he didn't seem happy.'

'Who was that?'

'Myra. Over at the saloon. She rode right in here with him – right in the surrey and all – then I heard this terrible row. And she slapped him.'

'You're sure it was Myra?'

'Positive. It was one of them nights when none of the saloons was feelin' partial to me.' He shrugged. 'Some nights they're nicer than others. Anyway, I come back here early and got up in the loft and was just sort of playin' around with Mike over there – we really are pals, I'd have to say – and then I hear the surrey come in and there's your brother and Myra.'

'You saw her?'

'They was arguin', so I looked over the edge of the loft.'

'Could you hear what they were arguing about?'

'Not really. But she was awful mad. She let him have a couple of good ones.'

Payne stood up. He took a coin from his pocket and tossed it down to Rupert. 'Have one on me.'

'Thanks, mister.'

Chapter Eighteen

She sat a long time in Aunt Thea's front room, quietly rocking herself into a half-dream state, only vaguely hearing the traffic that jangled by in the street.

Aunt Thea had been gone for more than two hours.

She hadn't been sick for some time now, maybe as long as three hours. The afternoon now rolling toward dusk, the front room in which she sat was shadowy. She felt good in the shadows, as if she could hide in them forever.

A little while earlier, dozing here in the chair, she'd had a dream of the child again, a dream she did not want to have because she wasn't sure she was ready to be a mother yet, especially given the circumstances.

Her confusion had started to exhaust her.

She just wasn't sure what to do.

*   *   *

By the time Aunt Thea returned, near suppertime, Kate was asleep in the rocking chair.

Aunt Thea came over, put her hands on the young woman's shoulders, leaned down, and kissed her gently on the top of her head.

Kate had had such a difficult life. First, losing her parents in that terrible fire, and then bearing the mark of that fire with the burns on her face. And now becoming pregnant —

Aunt Thea put some tea on. When it was ready, and had been poured into a nice cup, she set bread and butter on a plate along with the tea and carried it all into the front room.

She sat across from Kate and said softly, 'Kate, honey, why don't you have some tea?'

Kate's eyes flew open. At first, she looked uncertain of where she was. Then she recognized Aunt Thea and smiled. 'Hi. Sorry I fell asleep.'

'Lord, child, why should you be sorry?'

'Oh, I should be up and doing some work or something.'

'You should be resting. Just the way you were.'

Kate picked up a knife and spread butter on her bread. The wheat bread tasted good. She'd had little to eat all day. She added honey to the second slice, making the bread taste even better.

Aunt Thea said, 'You come to any decision yet?'

Kate shook her head. She didn't want to start crying.

Aunt Thea held up her hand. 'Honey, I know what you're going through.'

Kate wanted to say, *No, you don't. You've never had children and* —

'I did the same thing you did when I was young.'

Kate almost choked on her bread. 'You did? Really?'

'Yes. He was a lieutenant in the army.' Aunt Thea smiled at the memory. Then the smile faded. 'He was in town two weeks. My mother thought it was scandalous, how much time I spent with him. And it was, too, I suppose.' Whenever Aunt Thea talked about her mother – who must have been a woman stern beyond belief – her jaw muscles began to work and sometimes Kate could see Aunt Thea's fingers begin to twitch involuntarily. 'Anyway, when he left, I was pregnant.'

'Did you tell your mother?'

'Oh, no, never. Not my mother.'

'Then what did you do?'

'Oh, I wrote my handsome lieutenant two letters and told him about my condition, but he never wrote back.'

'And so you —?'

Even in the dusky shadows, the tears standing in Aunt Thea's eyes were obvious. 'I married your uncle. He knew my situation and he knew I didn't love him' – a sweet, curious rapture came into her voice – 'but he was so good and decent, your uncle. He said, ''Someday you'll love me, Thea, someday you'll love me.'' '

'What happened to the child?'

Thea shrugged. 'Stillborn. I cried for three months.' She raised her eyes to Kate, 'I saw it as punishment, God punishing me for what I'd done, the child being born dead and all.'

'Did you try to have others?'

'We tried. Didn't do any good, though. I guess I saw that as God's punishment too.' She paused and stared through the shadows at Kate. 'Kate, you'll find a man to marry you. I'm sure of it. Just the way I found your uncle.'

She wanted to believe, oh how she wanted to believe, and so she said, 'You really think so, Aunt Thea? You really think so?'

Then Aunt Thea was coming across the room, big bulky body encircling Kate, and holding the young woman as they both had good cries.

Then Aunt Thea was in the kitchen, rattling pans, starting supper.

For a long time, Kate sat there transfixed. How simple and wonderful everything seemed at this moment – everything would be fine. She would find a man and —

And then her fingers touched her burned cheek, and she heard the laughter of her school days as she walked by a group of especially cruel little boys. . . .

She knew that things would not be all right. She would never find a husband.

All through supper, Aunt Thea kept asking Kate why she was so suddenly glum, and all Kate could do was give little shrugs and sighs.

Kate set down her teacup. 'I think I'd like to go for a walk. Would you mind?'

'Not at all.'

Kate got up and kissed Aunt Thea on the cheek.

'I'll be back in a little while.'

'There's a nice breeze. It's a beautiful night for a walk.'

Kate got her jacket from the front closet and went to the door. 'Thanks again for everything, Aunt Thea. I couldn't ask for a better friend.'

She went outside then. Aunt Thea hadn't been exaggerating. There was a bright quarter moon and the scent of autumn leaves and any number of companionable neighborhood dogs to keep her company on her walk.

Kate set off.

Chapter Nineteen

The first time Payne stopped in the saloon that afternoon, he was told that Myra wasn't feeling well and was sleeping. The second time he stopped, he was told that she'd gone off somewhere doing errands. This third time, Payne noticed that when the bartender said that Myra still wasn't back yet, his eyes flicked to the stairs leading to the second floor. The bartender wasn't good at lying.

Payne nodded, thanked the man, gulped down the last of his small glass of beer, then made his way through the chest-high haze of smoke to the batwing doors. With nightfall, the place was filling up fast. The girls, mostly farm girls, worked the tables where the men bragged and argued and played cards.

Outside, Payne stood beneath the overhang, thinking about what to do next. Actually, it seemed pretty simple.

An alley ran along the east side of the saloon. Payne walked over there, moving as if he were just out for an evening's amble, then went around back to where two very satisfied-looking grey cats sat atop two plump garbage cans. To the right of the garbage cans were steps leading to the second floor.

Payne glanced around and, not seeing anybody watching, started up the steps.

Halfway up, he used his good hand to take out his .44. He might need it.

Climbing the steps reminded him that he'd been wounded. The stairs sapped his strength. He knew he'd soon need to lie down. Even when the pain wasn't considerable, even when the sling rode nice and comfortable, he was still not as strong as he wanted or needed to be.

A screen door stood at the top of the steps. He peeked in. A long hallway ran the length of the second floor, with doors off to both the right and left. For now, the hallway was empty. Dusk made the place dark, except for a lantern sitting on a small table in the center of the hallway.

Payne eased the door open and went inside. The door made a small squawking sound, like a parrot that hadn't yet learned manners. He kept his .44 ready in his good hand.

He tiptoed down the hall, leaning his head left then right, trying to hear what went on behind the closed doors. He heard nothing. Apparently, most of the ladies were already downstairs, now that the night was here.

A rubber runner ran the length of hallway, sticky from splashed beer. The air was overwhelmed by lingering perfume.

The fourth door down on the right, he heard something: a woman singing. Nothing fancy, no trying to impress herself with her talent, just singing bits and pieces of a sentimental song to herself.

Payne recognized the song, 'Fly Back Home, My Darling,' and he recognized the woman: Myra.

He checked the hallway again and found nothing, so he leaned over and put his ear to the door. Still singing. He put the .44 in his bad hand for a moment and then tried the doorknob. It turned, unlocked.

There was only one way to go in, he figured, and that was straight in.

He eased open the doorknob, shifted the .44 back to his good hand, then pushed the door inward.

She sat at a dressing table, powdering her face in a round mirror. At first, the reflection of her once-beautiful face looked angry. Then she glanced down at the .44 in his hand and looked scared.

'Hello, Stephen.'

He kicked the door shut behind him. 'You were seeing my brother.'

She went back to putting on her powder. It was almost as if she hadn't heard him. Then she paused and raised her eyes to his in the mirror. 'I knew you'd find out.'

'You used to take rides with him in a surrey.'

'I didn't realize there was a law against that, Stephen.'

'You know about his death, then. You lied to me.'

This time she didn't glance at him at all. She just finished powdering her face and started daubing on perfume. She wore a low-cut blue organdy dress. The tops of her breasts looked fetching, even now. 'I really don't, Stephen. Know anything, I mean. And if you don't believe me —

Payne saw it then and realized he'd been suckered. There was a tall, narrow closet to the left of the door. A trembling went through the heavy green curtain. Somebody was in the closet. Somebody who had a gun pointed directly at Payne's head.

A man came out, big and rough in cowboy clothes that were too fancy by half, especially the black ten-gallon hat that only Easterners would be impressed with.

Payne watched the man in the mirror.

He came out of the closet and straight for Payne. He put the barrel of the gun right to Payne's head and said, 'I'd just as soon shoot you. Nothin' personal, mister, it's just the way I am.'

'He's not fooling, Stephen.' She smiled at the man in the mirror. 'He's not quite right in the head and he's the bloodiest bastard I've ever known.'

'Now you go real quiet, mister,' the man said, 'or I'm going to put a big hole right in the middle of your head.'

But Payne was too mad for the moment to listen. 'I thought we were friends, Myra.'

She raised her gaze in the glass, and for the first time he saw her rage. 'Friends? The way you walked out on me? Not likely, Stephen. Not goddamn likely at all.'

'Who killed my brother, Myra?'

'Earle, I'm getting tired of him. Get him out of here.'

The funny thing was, Earle didn't need a gun. He had this outsize left hand, and he took it and clamped down on Payne's wounded shoulder and squeezed. That was all it took.

Payne heard himself scream, then saw cold rushing darkness start to pull him down, then felt Earle clamp down again.

And again, Payne screamed.

'That's enough, Earle. Just get him out of here, if you don't mind.'

Payne was barely aware of being hustled out, shoved through the door, pushed down the hallway, and thrown through the screen door. He stumbled down the steps to the dusty alley and flailed toward it as he started to fall.

He wasn't out long, maybe ten minutes at most. When he came to, he found that two cats stood on either side of his head taking curious note of this odd human being who couldn't even walk down a flight of stairs by himself.

But all he could think of was Myra; how she'd spent so much time with Art, how Myra surely knew what had happened to his younger brother during the last terrible days of his life.

Chapter Twenty

Clinton Todd was dreaming of a woman. His new woman. That was the trouble with women, they got familiar and boring too quickly. They began to say the same things over and over, began to react to things in predictable ways, began to ask for more than he could possibly give them, considering the fact that he was a married man and an exceedingly respectable citizen. No, the beginning was always the best. Firm new bodies, surprising new minds.

He was sitting in his office, in the big leather chair usually reserved for clients, dreaming about his latest lover and how in just a few hours he'd see her, when he heard a faint, timid knock on his door.

Who the hell would that be? he wondered.

He got up and found out.

She had been walking down the boardwalk, when on impulse, she headed toward Clinton's office – though she supposed she shouldn't even have been doing that. Suddenly she found her hand on the doorknob. Pushing into the dark interior. Going up the steps. Heart hammering. Sickness threatening. At the top of the stairs, panic overwhelmed her. Taking two steps back down the steps. She felt like running away.

Instead, she returned to the top of the stairs and stood at the door of Clinton's office, raising her small hand and hearing the hard hollow sound as she knocked.

Clinton stood there in the doorway, clearly angry. 'Do you have any idea how busy I am?'

'I'm sorry, Clinton.'

'Then if you're sorry, why the hell did you come here?'

'I just thought I'd better tell you.'

'Tell me what, for Christ's sake?'

'That I'm pregnant.'

There. It was said. She didn't care what happened now, didn't really expect any consolation whatsoever from him. She'd just wanted to see his face, just hear his first words.

He said, 'Oh, great, that's all I need. As if I don't have enough goddamn things to worry about.'

And she laughed.

She knew she sounded crazy, but laughter was the only response that seemed appropriate right now. Because his answer had been so, so – well, so *Clinton*. Totally self-absorbed.

'What the hell's so funny?'

'You.'

'Well, thank you.'

'And me. I mean, I guess I'm just as funny as you arc, Clinton.'

'What the hell are you talking about, Kate?'

'You'd never understand, Clinton.'

He looked at her, some of his handsomeness lost in the sourness of his expression. 'I suppose you want money.'

'I don't want anything, Clinton.'

'Then why the hell bother me with it at all?'

And then she couldn't help herself – maybe she really was crazy – but just as easily as the laughter had come, now came tears. 'Because I'm carrying a life inside me, Clinton, and I just thought you might be interested!'

More tears than she knew what to do with. More humiliation than she knew what to do with.

She wanted to leave, but she felt immobilized.

His hands on her shoulders, saying, 'I don't want you to think I'm an ass, Kate.'

The laughter again. The crazy laughter, mixed now with her tears. She felt drunk, groggy, dreamy. 'Oh, no, Clinton, I'd never think that.'

'I just have a lot of pressures on me, Kate, and sometimes I suppose I seem – insensitive.'

'That's it, Clinton. Pressures.'

'This has happened to me before, Kate, a baby like this, I mean. You can always go away and have the child, then give it to somebody.'

She was stunned by how easily he dismissed the child, their child.

'Would two hundred dollars help?' he asked in response to her silence.

'No, thanks.'

'Would —'

She held up her hand to stop him. She was regaining her poise. 'I really shouldn't have come here, Clinton.'

'I'm sorry about all this, Kate. I really am.' He hesitated. 'Kate, I have to ask you something.'

'I know what you're going to say, Clinton.'

'You do?'

'You're going to ask me not to tell anybody.'

'Well —'

'And I won't. Remember, it's my reputation, too.'

'You're really a very nice girl, Kate.'

And so there it was.

'I think I'm going to be sick, Clinton.'

'Huh?' Then he realized what she meant by sick. 'My wife was that way with our three boys. Sick all the time.'

'Please, Clinton, I have to go.'

'I really would give you some money, Kate.'

She shook her head.

Before she reached the stairway she was sick. She threw up in a cleaning bucket in the hallway. Clinton surprised her by coming over and standing by her.

When she was finished, she looked up at him. She felt horrible, undignified.

Then, before she knew what was happening, he was

holding money out to her, greenbacks that crinkled in the stillness.'

'You know who Helga is,' he said. And he was right. Everybody knew who Helga was. And what she did. 'You take this to Helga tonight. She'll take care of you. And then you won't have any more problems.'

He pushed the money into her hand, then turned and was gone. He closed his office door very quietly.

A big male hand came out of the darkness and gently took her arm.

Charlie didn't say anything, just walked her downstairs to the front door, then went back down the first-floor hall to his own cubbyhole. When he came back he carried two sticks of chewing gum. 'It's Adam's Tutti-Frutti. It's my favorite.'

She took a stick, thanked him, and they went outside and sat on the front stoop.

'I suppose you heard us.'

'Guess I did,' he said.

'So you know about the baby.'

'Guess I do.'

'You know about Helga?'

He looked over at her, his wrinkled face sad. 'I know her pretty good. She's a nice lady.'

'She is?'

'Uh-huh. And clean and careful, too.'

'I'm glad to hear you say that.'

For a time they didn't talk, just sat and listened to the early evening, the distant dogs and distant excited kids, the wagons rolling down the dusty street, the sentimental sounds somewhere of a fiddle just as the stars were appearing in the hazy dusk sky.

'You think it's a good idea, Charlie?'

'Helga?'

'Uh-huh.'

'Can't say. Only you can say.'

'I'm scared.'

'I know. I wish I could help you.'

'I was so stupid, Charlie.'

'He's got charm. Unfortunately.'

'He sure does, Charlie.' She frowned. 'You really hate him, huh?'

'Way he treats me – way he treats his women – yes, I hate him.'

'Why do you stay?'

Charlie shrugged. 'An old man who's a Cherokee besides? Not a lot of jobs around.'

'How about the reservations?'

Charlie shook his head, his greying hair almost white in the dusk light. 'Too much bitterness. I know why they're bitter, but that doesn't make it any easier to be around.' Then Charlie looked up and said, 'Oh – oh.'

'What?'

'His new lady.'

'Where?'

Charlie nodded down the boardwalk to the east. 'Looking all spruced up and ready for a big night.'

'I don't want to see her again, Charlie. She's too beautiful.'

'C'mon.' He took her hand and helped her up.

140

He led her around to the alley.

They stood against the building. Then Charlie peeked around the corner and began describing the woman's progress not unlike a horse race. 'Here she comes. She's gittin' close now.'

'How's she look?'

'Oh, not all that good.'

'I'll bet. I'll bet she's beautiful.'

'She's about ten yards away now. Whoops.'

With that, Charlie jerked his head back and pressed himself against the building. He put a finger to his lips, and for two long, heart-thudding moments they listened as the front door opened and dainty footsteps flew up the stairs.

The rest of it, Kate didn't hear. And she certainly didn't want to imagine.

'Well,' Charlie said, 'I guess I'd better get back to work. Still got six offices to go tonight.'

Kate leaned over and kissed him on the cheek. 'I'm sorry I had to use your bucket upstairs, Charlie. You sure are nice to me,' she said.

'Well, you're a nice girl.'

She smiled sadly. 'Yes, that's just what Clinton said.'

Charlie laughed. 'But I mean it.'

She laughed also and walked him around to the front of the building, then left.

Chapter Twenty-one

Lantern light cast long shadows down the narrow hotel corridor. Payne was on his way to his room. He'd been to a lot of places today and was exhausted.

Just as he took his room key from his pocket, he thought he saw the door across from his room open, then close quickly. But maybe the dim light just had him imagining things.

He put the key in his door and went inside, closing the door behind him.

He went straight to the bed, sat on the edge, and took his boots off. Not easy, because of his sore shoulder. Next he unhooked his gun rigging and set it on the floor. He propped the pillow up so that he could lie against the wall and doze off. Sleeping on his stomach or side was too difficult with his wound.

He got as comfortable as possible and took his last look at the room for a while – the starlit sky in the window, the dark shape of the bureau in the corner, the closed closet door to his left, a straight-back chair next to it. He'd been in a hundred hotel rooms like this. He could only hope that he wouldn't end up one of those old men who die out their time in such places.

He closed his eyes. Sleep took him quickly, almost tenderly, his senses shutting down, his mind drifting into cosmic darkness.

Then he smelled it.

Five years ago, riding across a winter plain, a blizzard had killed his horse and forced Payne to scramble for shelter. All he'd been able to find was a shallow cave carved in ragged rock. As he approached the dark mouth, a singular odor overwhelmed him. He wouldn't have called the odor unpleasant exactly, but the smell did seem to be tainted with a hint of something unclean. At the time, he had no idea what the smell was. But as soon as he took two steps into the cave, he saw right away what caused the stench. Rattlers, maybe a dozen of them, entwined on the dirt floor of the cave, seeking shelter from the blizzard just as their human brother was. He'd never forgotten the odor; whenever a smart-ass tried to tell him that rattlers had no odor, Payne just smiled to himself. There was no arguing with fools.

Now, propped up against the wall, he smelled the rattler and opened his eyes.

The snake was coiled in the center of the bed. In the shadows, it looked mostly black, though pale moonlight painted a patch of earth-colored diamondback flesh.

Payne tried to move his hand away.

The rattler hissed and wound closer to him.

Payne left his hand still. Very still.

Moments later, the snake's tail began to rattle and Payne realized that the odds were good the snake would strike. Most times they wouldn't, but sometimes, especially if their venom needed to be spent, they could be very deadly.

Payne was scared.

His stomach, his bowels, and his heart all seemed to draw in on themselves. Icy sweat rolled down his face in crystal bubbles. His mouth was so dry he wasn't sure he could even cry out.

He dangled his right hand off the edge of the bed.

Maybe he could lean over and very stealthily pick up his .44 and —

His right hand dangled in dark emptiness.

There was no way he could ever bend over that far without alarming the snake.

As if to prove this, the snake's rattle sounded again, loud and lurid in the dusty hotel room.

The smell grew stronger as the snake inched closer.

My God. To just have to sit here and wait and —

He thought of heaving himself off the bed, but he knew that with his wound and his exhaustion, he'd never be quick enough. He'd move and the rattler would move and —

Somebody knocked.

The sound was startling. At first, Payne was so caught up in his fear he barely recognized the knock for what it was.

But his eyes raised slowly to the door. 'Yes?' he said, gaze flickering back to the snake as it drew even nearer.

'It's me, Kate. May I come in? You sound kind of funny, Payne. Are you all right?'

And then, without waiting for an answer, she pushed the door open and came in.

'Payne?'

Her eyes had not yet adjusted to the room's darkness.

'I'm on the bed. Over here.'

She peered through the murk.

The snake rattled its tail.

'Payne, what's that noise?'

'Rattler.' He was muttering.

'What?'

'Rattlesnake.'

'On your bed?'

'Uh-huh.'

'My God.'

She had been steadily inching her way over to the bed, but now she stopped as the snake hissed once more.

'Did it bite you?'

'Not yet. But any moment now.'

She glanced around the room. It was still difficult to see things in this room, especially when she was trembling as hard as she was. She had an almost immobilizing fear of snakes.

She saw the chair next to the bureau. 'Hold on, Payne.'

'Not much else I can do right now.'

She eased over by the window and picked up the chair. She could use the legs to fight the snake off.

She tiptoed back over to the bed and got her first good look at the reptile in the moonlight. It was no more than six inches from Payne's arm, coiling and uncoiling, hissing and rattling, sounding angry.

Repulsed by the sight of the snake, she shuddered.

'Here goes,' she said.

She pushed the legs of the chair directly at the rattler. It obliged her by striking directly at one of the chair's legs.

In the moonlight, she could see its tongue slashing out at the chair and its agile body snap whiplike in her direction.

Payne rolled off the bed, jumped to his feet, and ran around behind her, heading directly for – the snake.

'Payne, what're you doing?'

'I'm afraid this old boy isn't done working for the night.'

'What're you talking about, Payne?' She had the discomfiting thought that maybe the snake had already bitten Payne, and that the man was now brain-addled from the venom.

Payne knew what he was doing.

He eased his way up to the bed, then lunged forward

with amazing speed, his good hand grasping the snake right behind its head.

The hissing and rattling started up again, but Payne didn't seem at all impressed. He just held on tight to the snake, walked across the room, went through the open door, and stepped into the hallway.

Without looking in either direction, he walked over to the room directly across from his, bent down, cracked the door open an inch or so, and flung the rattler inside.

He came right back to his own room, closed the door about halfway, and whispered, 'Now we wait.'

'Will you tell me what's going on?'

'Keep your voice down.'

'Why'd you throw that snake into the room across the hall.'

'Just hold on, Kate. You'll see.'

They didn't have to wait long in the darkness.

A few moments later they heard a man yell, 'The sonofabitch threw the rattler in here!'

Then Kate and Payne heard the sound of furniture being knocked over in the room across the hall as the two men scrambled to get out of the rattler's way.

'Dammit, Haskins, can't you get a shot at this pecker?'

'Me? How about you, Cooley? You're supposed to be the ace shot!'

Then Haskins let out a squeal. 'I can hear it rattlin', Cooley. It's right next to my foot.'

'Well, shoot it, you fool, shoot it!'

And then, dutifully, came the bark of two gunshots in the gloom.

While the blasts were still echoing in the hotel hallway, Payne eased himself out the door, into the hallway again.

He pressed himself against the wall just to the right of their door and waited.

He didn't have to wait long. When the first man came out Payne thumbed the hammer back on his .44 and put the gun barrel right against Haskins' temple.

His partner came right behind.

'You take one more step,' Payne said, 'and I'll kill him. You understand?'

Cooley nodded.

'Who hired you to put a snake in my room?'

'What snake?' Cooley said.

'You want to see your friend dead?' Payne said, jamming the gun once again against Haskins's temple. 'It was Clinton Todd, wasn't it?'

'No,' Cooley said.

'Yes, it was, mister,' Haskins said, sounding as if he was about to cry. 'It was definitely Clinton Todd.'

Payne hit Haskins with a sudden savagery that shocked and intimidated Cooley, who leaned over and grabbed his friend under the arms before he fell to the floor.

'You maybe killed him, mister.'

'Yeah, maybe I did.'

'You had no call to do that.'

'Sure, I did. I should kill you both for putting the

148

rattler in my room.' Payne lowered his .44 and crossed the hallway to his own room. He went in and closed the door.

'You hit that man pretty hard, huh?' Kate said.

'Yeah, I guess I did.'

Payne opened the door and looked into the hall.

Cooley had Haskins propped up against the wall. Haskins had his eyes open and was talking. Despite the trickle of blood down his face, he looked to be all right.

'He's alive,' Payne said.

'Good,' she said.

He closed the door again. 'You got any idea how I could get into Clinton Todd's office?'

'Why would you want to do that?'

'Because I'll bet that among his papers I'll find something that will tie him to my brother's death.'

'You sure?'

'He just tried to have me killed, didn't he? I'd say that sounds like he's got something to hide.'

She didn't say anything for a time. 'You're different now, harsh and hard the way men get when they go crazy.'

He realized she was right. The snake had scared him so much that rage had taken him over completely. He trembled, and his voice was deeper, and he wished he had two good hands so he could set about smashing something in, somebody's face or a wall – right at this moment it didn't much matter.

'Will you help me get into Todd's office?'

'If you'll be like you were before, I will.'

149

He was almost unaware of what he did next, taking her hand and guiding her up from the bed and into his arms.

He kissed her hard the first time, then realized that the kiss was just another expression of his rage, so then he kissed her soft. He felt a tenderness that was balm to his wounds, both the physical and the spiritual ones, and when he was done kissing her he held her gently in his arms, his good hand caressing the shape of her head, the soft dark hair, the sweet tender hollow of her cheek.

'Does it make you feel funny?' she asked.

'Huh?'

'Touching my cheek.'

And only then did he realize he was touching her burned cheek.

'No,' he said, 'it doesn't make me feel funny at all.'

'I'm glad it's dark in here.'

'You are?'

'It's nice in the darkness because then I don't have to worry about my face.'

He heard years of shame in her voice. 'You've got a fine face, Kate.'

'Not the burned part.'

'Maybe you notice it more than others do.'

'Maybe.' She sighed. 'That's why I let Clinton make love to me. I thought if a man that fine-looking and that respectable and that prominent wanted to make love to me – well, I figured I must be all right then.' She sighed again. 'I'm supposed to see Helga tonight.'

150

'Helga?'

'She helps women like me.' She paused. 'Do you understand what I'm saying?' He nodded.

'I don't know what to do, Payne.'

Payne knew what he wanted to say, but it wasn't his business to tell her what to do.

Besides, despite the respite her kiss had provided him, the rage was back.

'Can you help me, Kate? I've got to get into Todd's office.'

'I can ask Charlie to help us.'

'You think he will?'

'I think he will.'

Payne got his hat and jacket, and they went out into the hall.

Haskins was standing up now. He looked unsteady, but he also looked all right. He scowled at Payne. 'You didn't have no call to coldcock me like that.'

'I guess I didn't. But I didn't appreciate the rattler, either.'

Haskins dropped his eyes, looking embarrassed now.

Payne and Kate walked past Cooley, on down the hall, and down the stairs to the lobby.

151

Chapter Twenty-two

This time they met in the bank.

At night the arched ceiling and the wide, open expanse of floor lent the place the air of a church, as if parishioners might come here literally to worship money. The teller cages, lost mostly now to evening shadows, might have been confessionals where the penitent came to confess that worst sin of all: *I don't have any money*. And the bank vault? Well, that's where the Almighty itself lived, away from grubby human hands and even grubbier human dreams.

They were in McCarthy's own office in the rear of the building, a plush place of flocked wallpaper, leather furniture, and beautiful mahogany inlay.

'A damned rattlesnake?' Sheriff Reeves said.

Where the lawman's response was bluster, McCarthy's response seemed to be a form of coma. He was sitting in his chair behind his fancy desk when Clinton

Todd told him what he'd done, hiring Cooley and Haskins to put the snake in Payne's bed; McCarthy's head just fell forward and his eyes closed. He shook his head – slowly, mournfully, over and over and over again.

'Goddamn sonofabitch,' Sheriff Reeves said, being one of those men for whom swearing seemed to offer solace. 'Where is Payne now?'

Clinton Todd, like a scolded boy, barely whispered. 'I don't know.'

'Well, he's now survived two attempts on his life, and he's gonna be a whole lot madder than he was, and he was already madder than hell,' the lawman said. He waited a moment, then slammed his fist against the surface of McCarthy's desk. 'Clinton, what the hell were you thinking of?'

'I'm too old to go to prison,' McCarthy said, seeming to revive now that he'd sipped his sherry.

'Sonofabitch!' Sheriff Reeves said again.

'He'll probably leave,' Clinton Todd said.

'Oh, sure, Clinton,' McCarthy said, picking up on some of the lawman's sarcasm. 'He survives a shooting and a run-in with a rattlesnake, and then he just decides to leave.'

Reeves said, 'He's gonna keep on askin' questions, Clinton, and you damn well know it.'

'And eventually,' McCarthy said, 'he's gonna get some answers, too.'

'And that's when our asses are really gonna be in a sling,' Sheriff Reeves said.

Clinton Todd got up and went over to one of the side windows. The shade had long ago been drawn, so he held it back some with his finger and peeked outside. He could see the stars, and they looked to him now as they had when he was a boy, mysterious and inviting. He hadn't thought about stars in a long time, and he realized that was one of the terrible things about becoming an adult. You lost your passion for the things that used to matter to you, like stars and secret caves and creeks filled with leaping bass.

He turned back to his two partners and said, 'Since you don't seem to have any stomach for how I've handled things the past few days, why don't you gentlemen suggest something? You seem to know everything about goddamn everything. Give me some of your wisdom, then.'

'Now, Clinton,' McCarthy said, 'don't go using that tone of voice with us. We're your friends, remember?'

'Well, the way you've been talking here tonight, I was beginning to wonder,' Todd said.

Reeves said, 'Sit down, Clinton. Fiery balls, nobody here is castigatin' anybody for anything. We know you did your best.'

Clinton Todd covered his face with his hands, shutting out the light. If he closed his eyes, Reeves and McCarthy weren't sitting in this office and Stephen Payne wasn't presenting him with a terrible problem. All he had to do was keep his eyes closed.

Reeves said, 'You with us, Clinton?'

Todd sighed, opened his eyes, and lowered his hands.

Suddenly he realized what he was going to do. He wasn't going to tell either of these frightened old men what he had in mind, and he wasn't going to worry about the consequences, because later on, when Reeves needed to know what had happened – that Clinton had gone and shot Payne himself – well then, things could be fixed and nobody in town would ever know, and Favor would be just the way it was before Payne had ridden in three days ago.

'Clinton? You all right?' McCarthy said.

'I'm fine.'

'You look kind of – sickly or something.'

'I'm fine. Really.'

'All right, then,' McCarthy said, looking at his fellow conspirators, 'now, we've got to make some plans.'

The meeting went an hour longer, and they didn't come up with a single scheme.

But Todd didn't care. His plan was simple and direct, and he was going to put it into action in just an hour or two.

Chapter Twenty-three

Kate raised a hand and knocked lightly on the glass. Before reaching the door, she'd looked upstairs to make sure that Clinton's office was dark.

'Maybe Charlie's gone home,' Payne said.

'Maybe.'

'I doubt he'd want to help us anyway.'

'He might surprise you.'

She turned back to the front door and knocked again. The dusty street was dark, the brick buildings and false fronts looming in moon-tinted shadows.

Far inside, as if from the very bowels of the basement, came a sound that vaguely resembled a human voice.

Kate cupped her hands to the sides of her eyes so she could see better and peered deep into the dark tunnel of the first-floor hallway.

'It's Charlie,' she said, sounding exultant.

Payne smiled at her fleeting joy.

Charlie opened the door. Even in the shadows, Kate could see the whorls of his face.

'Charlie, this is Stephen Payne.'

'Nice to meet you,' Payne said and shook hands with the man.

'Heard about somebody tryin' to shoot you,' Charlie said. 'Favor's usually a friendlier town than that.'

'Tonight somebody put a rattlesnake in his bed,' Kate said.

Charlie shook his head and frowned.

Kate said, deciding to just get it over with, 'Charlie, do you think you could arrange for Stephen to get into Clinton's office?'

'You mean tonight?'

'Right now, Charlie.'

'Oh, girl, that's a real serious thing you're asking me to do.'

'I know, Charlie, and I wouldn't ask you except Stephen doesn't have any other way to find out how his brother really died.'

Charlie leaned on his broom and stared at Payne. 'You think Todd had something to do with it?'

'Yes, I do.'

'If you found the right thing in his office, it might lead him to prison?'

'That's a possibility.'

'Is it also a possibility that Todd could get himself hanged?'

'I suppose it's possible.'

'Good,' Charlie said gleefully. 'Then I'll help you.'

Payne laughed. 'I appreciate this.'

'You two come on inside now,' Charlie said.

'Not me,' Kate said. 'I've got something I've got to do, Charlie.' She looked up at Payne. She could tell he was thinking about her going to Helga's, but he said nothing.

'Will you come and see me at my aunt's later tonight?'

Payne nodded, abruptly drew her to him, and kissed her gently on the forehead. 'You just be careful.'

'I will,' Kate said. 'I will.' Then she was gone into the long shadows of the night, no longer visible to him in the cool darkness.

'Nice young lady,' Charlie said.

'She sure is that,' Payne replied.

Then they went inside and got to work.

'I'll be downstairs,' Charlie said five minutes later. 'If I hear anybody coming, I'll pound on the floor three times with my broom handle, you got that?'

Payne nodded.

'And whatever you do, don't knock something over and break it. That Clinton Todd can be one mean sonofabitch, let me tell you.'

They were on the second floor, just outside Todd's door. The hallways smelled clean: Charlie had just finished sweeping and dusting.

Charlie bent over, inserted his key into the lock, wiggled it once – most keys have some sort of idiosyncrasy – and pushed the door open into the dark office.

'How you gonna see?'

'Guess I'll have to hold whatever I find up to the moonlight at the window.'

'Just remember.'

'I know. Three knocks of your broom handle.'

'Exactly.' Charlie shook his aged head again. 'And remember not to do nothin' that would cause Todd to kick my ass, because that's just what he'd like to do.'

Payne went inside.

He'd had no idea how dark it was going to be in here.

The very first thing he did was bump into a straight-back chair and knock it over on its side.

He could just hear Charlie cursing him already.

Chapter Twenty-four

Down by the river and just across the tracks, the world of Favor became a different place. Here the gypsies, poorer even than many of the blacks and Indians who lived on the periphery of Favor, lived in the colorful, decorative wagons that their people had pulled across Europe and down through the centuries to this new land where they were despised just as much as they'd been in the old lands. Seen close up, these wagons were just as battered as the people who drove them. Now, even in the moonlight, the wagons looked pale-faded and chipped and grimy in a way water could not help; the air smelled different, too, with mixed aromas from herbs the gypsies believed could cure everything from the common cold to deadly tumors. There were the strains of gypsy music, dark and bedeviled tunes played with curious sweetness on a guitar; in the windows of the six two-story houses where the older gypsies lived, people stood with their elbows leaning on windowsills, as aged eyes searched the starry night – for the gypsies believed that great dramas were played out in the skies, dramas that often foretold the future.

Kate slipped among the shadows, hurrying, afraid that if she slowed down she might change her mind. She wondered again how just a month ago she could have been so happy with Clinton – and he with her? She thought of how tenderly he would take her small face in his big hands, never showing any awareness of her burned cheek at all, and kiss her with such care. Had he only been fooling her? Was she truly not worthy of love, as she so often feared?

From the stoop of a house, an old gypsy called out a greeting she could not understand and hoisted the cup he was drinking from.

She hurried. The house she wanted was the last in the row. It was so dark here, she was afraid that she would trip and fall. She was also afraid that she might get sick again

The guitar music faded behind her and the rush of the river grew louder. The nearer she got to the end of this solitary row of houses, the more foreign the neighborhood seemed. Since childhood on, she'd been told stories of this place, imprecise stories to be sure, but ones that hinted at secrets good Christian people shunned.

She went up to the door and knocked. Almost immediately the door was flung open, and there in a beam of yellow light that extended all the way to the grass stood a tall woman in a ruffled peasant blouse, long cotton skirt, and clacking bracelets on her arm.

'Good evening,' the woman said.

'Good evening.'

'You are looking for Helga?'

'Yes – ' Kate waved the greenbacks. 'Clinton Todd told me.'

'Oh, yes, Clinton,' the woman said, a smile evident in her voice. It was an ironic smile, not without contempt. She held out her hand. 'But it is not Clinton we are worried about. It is you. Your health and your state of mind.'

Kate felt better already. She'd imagined that the woman would be grim and dour. This woman almost seemed to be laughing.

The interior of the two-story house was furnished with crude wooden furniture. Huge gaudy pillows lay on the floor for sitting, and in the center of a low table set in the exact middle of the room was a cloth-covered object that Kate took to be a crystal ball.

'I will get you some tea.'

'No, that's all right. I'm fine.'

The woman shook her head. She had a huge wart just above the left side of her lip. Her eyes shone like black diamonds. Her smile was rich and implied a hundred conflicting emotions. 'You don't understand, my child. The tea is for later, the operation.'

'Oh.'

'So you will please drink it?'

Kate nodded.

As she waited for the woman to return from the doorway to the right, she noticed the doorway to the left. Red, green and blue beads hung from the doorway, sparkling now in the flickering light of the lantern. Darkness lay beyond this door, but Kate knew instinctively that it was the room where the operation would be done.

She turned quickly away, bringing her attention back to the gypsy woman who had returned with two small cups of tea.

Kate accepted her cup along with the woman's admonition to drink it up.

'Your face,' the woman said. 'It is burned?'

'Yes. I was in a fire when I was young. My parents were killed.'

'I'm sorry. You're so pretty. And so quiet. And now you have another problem.'

'Yes.'

'Then it is just as well that it be done.'

'Yes.'

The woman studied her for a moment. 'You have doubts, however.'

'Some, I suppose.'

'The pain is not so much.'

'Good.'

'After a few days in bed you will feel good again.'

'I look forward to that.'

She noticed the dizziness then. It had come so suddenly.

'This tea . . . ?'

163

'It is meant only to relax you. Don't be afraid. The first sensations are a little unnerving, but then you will feel a wonderful well being.'

And so, just as the gypsy spoke, Kate did indeed begin to feel better.

The woman smiled. 'Sometimes the women like it so much that they come back afterward and ask for more of the tea.' She wagged her head. 'But this is a special tea. It can be used for no other occasion.'

Kate relaxed visibly, leaning back on the great gaudy pillow.

'You stay there, my child. I'll go get Helga.'

'You're not Helga?'

'Oh, no, child. Someday I would hope to know the things Helga knows and to be as respected in the community of gypsies as Helga is, but no, no, I am not Helga.'

And with that, she stood up and went through the clacking beaded doorway and into the darkness.

A lantern was lit. The beads sparkled.

A small, squat woman came through the beads. She was dressed in what appeared to be a grey woollen dress, severe for a spring night.

The woman came over and reached out her hand.

The other woman nodded for Kate to take Helga's hand. Kate complied. Helga had a hand strong as a man's. When she smiled, Kate saw that she had no teeth.

'Helga is happy to meet you. She says you look like a wonderful girl.' Then the gypsy woman leaned toward Kate and said, 'Helga cannot speak. When she was a young girl, some men raided her father's camp. They killed all the adults, then cut the tongues out of the children. They did this, they said, because gypsies tell only lies.'

Helga helped Kate to her feet.

Kate looked at the room ahead of her and felt Helga's strong hand around hers.

Chapter Twenty-five

Several times during his search of Clinton Todd's office, Payne thought he heard the faint sound of tapping on the floor beneath, but he was mistaken.

The search wasn't easy. Not in the darkness. Not with only one good hand.

But he continued to search anyway. He just had the sense that he would find something here. . . .

So he kept at it in the large, moonlit room, quietly going through drawer after drawer, filing cabinet after filing cabinet, holding up to the moonlight anything that looked promising.

He kept on. . . .

Todd went to Payne's hotel first. The desk clerk said that Payne had left some time ago.

Todd demanded the room key anyway. In this town,

only a handful of people had the power to refuse Clinton Todd.

He searched Payne's room and found little more than a frayed carpetbag and a few extra clothes. No doubt about it, the man was a worthless drifter.

Todd slammed the door and went down the stairs two at a time. He tossed the key to the clerk, then walked out into the street.

He was going to start checking the saloons. . . .

Payne barely heard the knock, but hearing it, he froze.

Had somebody gotten past Charlie and snuck up the stairs?

His good hand dropped to his gun.

His heart was beating so fast, he felt his chest constrict. Then, 'You gonna be in there much longer, mister? I think we about pushed our luck as far as we can.'

It was Charlie, peeking in through the partially opened door.

'Just a few more minutes,' Payne said.

Charlie shook his head, obviously not liking Payne's reply, but granting him the extra time.

Charlie's head vanished. The door closed.

The steps squeaked and groaned as he walked back down.

Payne started looking through the files again.

'He looked pretty mad,' Sheriff Reeves told the banker.

'He wouldn't do anything foolish.'

'The hell he wouldn't.'

'You think we should go try to find him?'

'That's what I been tryin' to tell you for the past half hour.'

'I sure hope he doesn't do anything crazy,' McCarthy said.

They left the bank by the back door and went in search of Clinton Todd.

Clinton Todd rarely went to the saloons. Tonight he didn't have any choice.

He went in all of them, searching for Payne.

They were filled with low-lifes and half-breeds and whores, most of whom smirked at him.

In his own sort of place, they would never dare smirk at Clinton Todd, Jr. He wouldn't let them.

But in this sort of place, where knives magically appeared in fingers and sliced sharp and deep across faces and torsos, Todd had no choice but to look the other way.

He had no luck finding Payne.

Chapter Twenty-six

Clinton Todd was walking down the street across from his office building when he saw Charlie come out the door and set down a wastepaper basket. Charlie usually lined them up on the boardwalk, then dragged one of the bins from the alley around to empty them.

But then something curious happened.

When Charlie glanced up and saw Todd, he ducked back into the building and closed the door.

Todd's curiosity led him to cross the street, to see just what the old Indian was up to.

This time there was no mistaking the sound.

Taps, tip-of-the-broom-handle-to-the-wooden-floor, three of them.

Fortunately Payne had already found what he'd been looking for. He had been searching for another document or two that would substantiate what he'd found when he heard Charlie's signal.

He slammed the filing cabinet door shut and stood up.

Dizzy. He was still weak from the wound, and his fevered search through the office here hadn't exactly made him any stronger.

He grasped the edge of a filing cabinet and held on to keep from pitching to the floor.

'What the hell's going on here?' Todd asked Charlie, who was standing at the foot of the stairs holding a broom.

'Huh?'

'Don't "huh?" me, you old bastard. Something's going on in here. Otherwise you wouldn't have tried to hide from me.'

'Didn't see you, sir,' Charlie said, knowing how white people liked to be called 'sir'. It was like giving them a birthday gift or something.

'The hell you didn't. Now let me up there.'

'Up there, sir?'

But Charlie had stalled and played dumb as long as he could.

Todd pushed him out of the way.

He took out his six-shooter and climbed the stairs three at a time.

The dizziness was just starting to recede when the office door opened and Clinton Todd came in, gun ready.

'You sonofabitch,' Todd said. 'That Indian bastard let you in here, didn't he?'

Before Payne could reply, Todd leaned over and got a kerosene lamp going.

Then he came over to Payne, lifted the .44 from Payne's holster, and laid it carefully on top of the filing cabinet.

That's when Todd saw the letter Payne had taken from the files.

'Well, well,' Todd said. 'So you figured it out, did you?'

Payne was standing straighter now, forcing deep breaths into his lungs. 'Art helped you rob the stage. You and Reeves and McCarthy were all in on it together, I imagine.'

'You're a lot smarter than you look, Payne,'

'You own a lot of land, but you don't have any cash. And the money that's in the bank belonged to the railroad —'

Then a voice interrupted him, a new voice.

Reeves and McCarthy came through the door. Reeves was speaking. 'We knew that when the railroad left, our little town would fold up and die. So we had to do something about that. We devised a plan where we hired somebody to stick up the stage when it was carrying the railroad payroll.'

'Making you all thieves,' Payne said.

McCarthy shook his head. 'That's the part you haven't figured out apparently. We didn't take the money for ourselves, son. We took it to give to the

171

Sterling Wagon Works so they'd relocate here. We had to do a whole lot of quick building before the wagon works would even consider relocating here – that's where the money went. And that's why we've still got a prospering town today.'

Reeves nodded. 'That's the truth, Payne. We were just being good citizens.' He smirked at Todd. 'Even Clinton, Jr. here, hard as that might be to believe.'

'Where did Art come in?' Payne said.

'We told him if he held up the stage for us, we'd give him two thousand dollars in greenbacks and safe conduct out of the Territory.'

'Then why would he hang himself?'

Reeves seemed genuinely sad. 'I don't know, Payne. I really don't. He did his part, he robbed the stage and left the money where we could get it. But he never met me that night for me to help him get away. The next morning we found out he had hanged himself. It don't make much sense, but I swear this is the truth.'

'I wonder what the stage line is going to think of all this when I tell them,' Payne said. He glared at Todd. 'I expect you'll do real well in prison, Todd.'

'Look, Payne,' Todd said. 'We never meant anyone harm, you or your brother.'

'What about Ken Briney? Which one of you hired him to try to kill me?'

'None of us,' Todd answered, looking from Payne to the sheriff and the banker. 'All right. I did pay a couple of men to scare you off with a rattlesnake, but I didn't have anything to do with Briney.'

McCarthy shook his head. 'Son, you ever heard of "for the greater good", when you do something you shouldn't so that others can benefit? That's all we did. Honest. We stole for the sake of the town – so that the whole town could prosper.'

Reeves pointed to the window. 'Out there are a lot of mighty fine folks, Mr Payne. You ain't been here long enough to know that, but it's true. They work hard, they go to church, they help their neighbors – and they were going to lose everything they had if we didn't help them.'

McCarthy said, 'And if you tell the stage line what happened – well, you won't just put us in prison, you'll put every one of those folks out there in the poorhouse. The truth is, the only way we could keep this town going was stolen money.'

Payne laughed harshly.

'I sure don't see anything funny in any of this,' McCarthy said.

'Well, I sure as hell do,' Payne said half-shouting, almost as if he were crazed. 'I can't do what's right – I can't tell the law what you boys have been up to – because if I do, I'll tear down a whole town.'

'Women and children,' Reeves said, seeing where Payne was going with his little speech.

'And old folks like me and maimed people,' McCarthy said. 'And blind people and deaf people and —'

'Shut up,' Payne said. 'I'm sick of you three.' He reached out, palm up, with his good hand.

'Give me my gun,' he said to Todd.

173

'Give it to him, Clinton. Give him his gun or I'll shoot you myself.'

Todd glowered, but put the handgun in Payne's palm.

'We're really sorry about your brother,' the banker muttered.

'I told you to shut up, McCarthy, and I meant it.'

Payne hefted his gun and started easing past the three men. He was sick of them, sick of the whole place. And anyway, he had other things to think about now.

He was remembering something Mrs Briney had said – how Briney had a mysterious late-night visitor. Then he thought of the surrey Art rented all those nights. Sure, he took Myra – but what if he also took somebody else on different nights?

'You going to turn us in, son?' McCarthy said, an old man's plea in his voice.

'I'd sure as hell like to,' Payne said. 'I sure as hell would.'

He glared at Todd once more, spat at his feet, then moved on out of the office.

Charlie met him on the first floor. 'Guess I'll be lookin' for another job.'

'Sorry, Charlie. But I appreciate everything.'

Then Payne set off into the night.

Chapter Twenty-seven

The grass had been cut that day, and the scent of new-mown blades lingered even now, at night.

The Todd house showed lights on every floor, with ruffled curtains in most windows and rich golden light just beyond. Life in such a place was unimaginable for somebody like Payne.

He went to the door and used the brass knocker.

In a minute or so, a round man in the formal attire of a butler appeared and said, 'Yes?'

'Mrs Todd, please.'

'I'm afraid it's awfully late.'

But from behind the man, Mrs Todd came to the door.

'Good evening, Mr Payne.'

'I'd like to talk to you.'

She glanced at him. He could see the beginnings of

fear in her eyes and along the lines of her mouth. But she said, 'Of course.'

The butler, looking none too pleased about admitting such a man, stood back and let Payne in.

The place had a parquet floor that stretched to the kitchen in the rear. To the left sprawled a huge living room. A fire snapped and popped in the brick fireplace.

'Why don't we use the den?' Mrs Todd suggested.

He followed her down the hall.

When she came to two large, sliding doors, she pushed one back and let him step inside.

Books lined all the walls. A massive rolltop desk dominated the entire east end of the room. A leather couch and matching chairs dominated the center of the room.

'Brandy, Mr Payne?'

'No, thanks.'

She watched him carefully a moment. 'You look angry.'

'Confused. Maybe later I'll be angry.'

'I see.'

He reached in his pocket and took the object he'd found in the box at the livery. He tossed it to her. It was an earring, solid gold. He hadn't understood the significance of it until he realized, back in Clinton Todd's office, that the three men hadn't killed his brother. Then the earring had given him an idea of who Art had been taking his surrey rides with.

'This is mine.'

'I know.'

'I lost it a long time ago.'

'You lost it on one of your late-night surrey rides with my brother.'

There. He'd said it. He could see from her face that his sudden suspicions were correct.

She went over to the liquor cabinet. She got out a cutglass brandy glass and filled it halfway up.

'Did you kill him, Mrs Todd?'

She turned around and came back. She seated herself in the center of the couch, across the room from him.

'You hired Briney to kill me. I assume that's because you had something to hide.'

She sipped brandy. Then she said, 'Do you believe in mercy, Mr Payne?'

'Sometimes.'

'I'm asking you for mercy now. For forgiveness.'

'If you mean Briney, you're forgiven. He missed and he's dead and I don't give a damn about him anymore. I just want the truth about Art.' He paused. 'He used to take you for surrey rides late at night, didn't he?'

'Yes. Your brother and I. . . .'

'Was he in love with you?'

'Yes. And I was in love with him. Very much in love with him.'

She reached into her pocket and took out a single sheet of paper.

She tossed it over to Payne.

'He wrote this to me the night before the robbery.'

Payne opened the letter. There was no mistaking

177

Art's bold scrawl. He read it quickly and set it down on the arm of his chair.

'You were going to go off with him and you backed out?'

'I don't expect you to understand or forgive me, Mr Payne.'

He realized then that she was crying.

'I came from humble circumstances, believe it or not. When I was seven years old, my mother sold me to a rich man as a servant girl. I got used to living in a big house, Mr Payne. I got used to a lot of things, thanks to the rich man. When he died I was nineteen years old and something of a beauty. I came west, ashamed of how I'd been living the past twelve years and wanting to start my life again. By then I was educated and poised and could pass myself off quite easily as wealthy. I met Clinton, and even though I saw him for the childish bastard he was, I knew he'd keep me in the manner I'd gotten used to.

'The funny thing is, I was never unfaithful until I met Art. I guess I saw in him the life I could have had – a lot more honest life than I'd been leading. We had been lovers for two years when he told me about the robbery and said that with the two thousand dollars we could run away together. Two thousand dollars sounded like a lot of money to him.

'The odd thing was, I not only told him that I would run off with him, I convinced myself that I would. We made plans – God, we spent so many nights taking those surrey rides and making plans – but when the actual moment came . . . I saw him the night before the robbery and told him that I couldn't go, I told him that I was too old now and too comfortable to leave my life, even though in many ways I really hated it.

'He couldn't believe it. First he got very angry, then he began sobbing, I don't think I've ever heard a man cry that way. I wanted to help him, but I couldn't. He went through with the robbery, but when he went to hide out in the barn —'

'He hanged himself,' Payne said.

'Yes,' she said, crying more herself now. 'Yes, that's just what he did.'

He sat and watched her. He didn't want to believe her, but he did. 'You tried to have me killed because you were afraid that my questions would let everybody in town know about your affair?'

'In my husband's world, men are permitted all the affairs they like. But a woman is thrown out if she so much as looks at another man.' She looked up at him with tears in her eyes. 'I really did love Art, Mr Payne, I really did.'

He sat there listening to the echoes of it all. Coming out here he'd thought that knowing the truth would somehow make him feel better about Art's death. But now, after reading Art's letter, after hearing Mrs Todd talk about the two of them —

Payne stood up.

Some of the dizziness came back.

'Are you all right, Mr Payne?'

'I'll make it.'

179

She stood up, too, and came to him and touched his arm. 'I'm sorry I have to ask you this but —'

He smiled sadly. 'Don't worry, Mrs Todd. I'm not going to tell your husband anything.'

'You're a very good man, Mr Payne. You really are. Art always said that, how good you were and how much he loved you and how he couldn't wait for me to meet you.'

Then it was Payne's turn to feel bitter tears in his eyes, to duck his head, to feel the coldness of his loss spreading through his body like an illness.

He wanted to go back in time and be a better friend, a better brother to Art, the kid he'd always taken for granted.

Then he was going down the hallway, Mrs Todd calling something out to him, something he no longer cared to hear, out into the dark moonstruck night.

Chapter Twenty-eight

The gypsy guitar was sad enough to match his mood.

He came riding the big dun at a gallop down the narrow dusty street, stopping at the last house. He had found Charlie and asked directions to Helga's.

He wasn't sure why, but now all that mattered was to see Kate. Not to hold her. Not even to speak to her. Just to see her. Because they were kindred souls, the two of them, and after he'd read Art's letter she was all he thought of.

He went up to Helga's door and knocked.

From the wagons to the west the guitar music continued; occasionally a baby cried and a dog barked.

A woman answered and he told her what he wanted.

She shook her head and did not speak, but pointed to the creek winding silver to the woods sloping high to the west.

He thanked her, confused, and mounted his dun once again.

It was ten minutes before he found Kate, sitting high on a boulder in the middle of the creek, skimming rocks along the surface of the shimmering water.

He ground-tied his dun and hurried down the slope to the creek, not hesitating to wade in deep so he could cross to her.

He put up his hand and she took it and said. 'I couldn't do it. I realized I didn't want to. . . .'

She came into his arms and he carried her back across the water. He cradled her, the child and the woman of her, and took her across the long grass to the dun. He set her high and safe on the saddle, then swung up himself and took the reins. Payne set off into the vast waiting night, loving her for the outcast she was and hoping she would some day love him for the outcast he was.

'Do you know where we're going?' she shouted into the wind, down from the mountains.

'No.'

'Do you know if we'll ever come back?'

'No.'

'Good,' she said, laughing, and hugged him all the tighter as a barn owl sang and the moon looked close enough to reach out and pluck from the midnight sky.

TROUBLE MAN

ED GORMAN

Ray Coyle used to be a gunfighter. And when he gets word his boy has been killed in a gunfight in Coopersville, he has to go there—to bring the body home. But when the old gunfighter steps off the train, he brings his gun with him, along with something else . . . trouble.

___4440-4 $4.99 US/$5.99 CAN

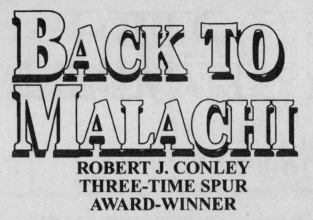

BACK TO MALACHI

ROBERT J. CONLEY
THREE-TIME SPUR
AWARD-WINNER

Charlie Black is a young half-breed caught between two worlds. He is drawn to the promise of the white man's wealth, but torn by his proud heritage as a Cherokee. Charlie's pretty young fiancée yearns for the respectability of a Christian marriage and baptized children. But Charlie can't forsake his two childhood friends, Mose and Henry Pathkiller, who live in the hills with an old full-blooded Indian named Malachi. When Mose runs afoul of the law, Charlie has to choose between the ways of his fiancée and those of his friends and forefathers. He has to choose between surrender and bloodshed.

___4277-0 $3.99 US/$4.99 CAN

THE GALLOWSMAN

WILL CADE

Ben Woolard is a man ready to start over. The life he's leaving behind is filled with ghosts and pain. He lost his wife and children, and his career as a Union spy during the war still doesn't sit quite right with him, even if the man sent to the gallows by his testimony was a murderer. But now Ben's finally sobered up, moved west to Colorado, and put the past behind him. But sometimes the past just won't stay buried. And, as Ben learns when folks start telling him that the man he saw hanged is alive and in town—sometimes those ghosts come back.

___4452-8 $4.50 US/$5.50 CAN

Dorchester Publishing Co., Inc.
P.O. Box 6640
Wayne, PA 19087-8640

Please add $1.75 for shipping and handling for the first book and $.50 for each book thereafter. NY, NYC, and PA residents, please add appropriate sales tax. No cash, stamps, or C.O.D.s. All orders shipped within 6 weeks via postal service book rate. Canadian orders require $2.00 extra postage and must be paid in U.S. dollars through a U.S. banking facility.

Name_____
Address_____
City_____ State_____ Zip_____
I have enclosed $_____ in payment for the checked book(s).
Payment <u>must</u> accompany all orders. ❏ Please send a free catalog.

LES SAVAGE, JR.
MEDICINE WHEEL

Bob Hogarth arrives in Wyoming's Big Horn Basin with nothing but a small herd of cattle, the result of stubborn scraping and saving back in Texas. He is determined to do better, to own his own ranch, to become a man of substance. But there are lots of folks who aren't too eager to see Hogarth succeed, other ranchers with their own plans for the future, and a mysterious rustler on a barefoot horse. Nobody told Hogarth his dreams would come easy . . . but he knows they are worth fighting for.

___4444-7 $4.50 US/$5.50 CAN

Dorchester Publishing Co., Inc.
P.O. Box 6640
Wayne, PA 19087-8640

Please add $1.75 for shipping and handling for the first book and $.50 for each book thereafter. NY, NYC, and PA residents, please add appropriate sales tax. No cash, stamps, or C.O.D.s. All orders shipped within 6 weeks via postal service book rate. Canadian orders require $2.00 extra postage and must be paid in U.S. dollars through a U.S. banking facility.

Name_____ _____
Address_____ _____
City_____ State_____ Zip_____
I have enclosed $_____ in payment for the checked book(s).
Payment <u>must</u> accompany all orders. ❏ Please send a free catalog.
CHECK OUT OUR WEBSITE! www.dorchesterpub.com

WILL HENRY

JOURNEY TO SHILOH

While the bloody War Between the States is ripping the country apart, Buck Burnet can only pray that the fighting will last until he can earn himself a share of the glory. Together with a ragtag band of youths who call themselves the Concho County Comanches, Buck sets out to drive the damn Yankees out of his beloved Confederacy. But the trail from the plains of Texas to the killing fields of Tennessee is full of danger. Buck and his comrades must fight the uncontrollable fury of nature and the unfathomable treachery of men. And when the brave Rebels finally meet up with their army, they must face the greatest challenge of all: a merciless battle against the forces of Grant and Sherman that will truly prove that war is hell.

_4203-7 $4.50 US/$5.50 CAN

WILL HENRY
CLASSIC TALES OF THE OLD WEST
AND ALL ITS GLORY!

The Crossing. Jud is the son and grandson of famous Southern generals. He was reared in the genteel Virginia traditions of his widowed mother, but life on a Texas ranch has molded him in the harsh ways of the frontier. In the deadly Confederate campaign to secure the region, Jud sees brave men fall with their guns blazing or die from naked fear. But he is of better stock than most, and he'll be damned if he'll betray the land—and the woman—he loves just to save his own worthless hide.

_4084-0 $4.99 US/$5.99 CAN

The Bear Paw Horses. Horse-thieving murderer Con Jenkins is thrown headfirst into the deadliest struggle of his life—a battle for the very horses that will bring the Sioux—or the white settlers—their greatest victory.

_4055-7 $4.99 US/$5.99 CAN

Dorchester Publishing Co., Inc.
P.O. Box 6640
Wayne, PA 19087-8640

Please add $1.75 for shipping and handling for the first book and $.50 for each book thereafter. NY, NYC, and PA residents, please add appropriate sales tax. No cash, stamps, or C.O.D.s. All orders shipped within 6 weeks via postal service book rate. Canadian orders require $2.00 extra postage and must be paid in U.S. dollars through a U.S. banking facility.

Name_____
Address_____
City_____ State_____ Zip_____
I have enclosed $_____ in payment for the checked book(s).
Payment <u>must</u> accompany all orders. ❑ Please send a free catalog.

WILL HENRY

ONE MORE RIVER TO CROSS

When Ned Huddleston stands up to a gang of small-town toughs, he trades his freedom for the harsh life of an outlaw. A wanted man, he flees west, where he discovers the song of the six-gun . . . and the ever-present shadow of the noose.

___4450-1 $4.50 US/$5.50 CAN

Dorchester Publishing Co., Inc.
P.O. Box 6640
Wayne, PA 19087-8640

Please add $1.75 for shipping and handling for the first book and $.50 for each book thereafter. NY, NYC, and PA residents, please add appropriate sales tax. No cash, stamps, or C.O.D.s. All orders shipped within 6 weeks via postal service book rate. Canadian orders require $2.00 extra postage and must be paid in U.S. dollars through a U.S. banking facility.

Name_____
Address_____
City_____ State_____ Zip_____
I have enclosed $_____ in payment for the checked book(s).
Payment <u>must</u> accompany all orders. ❏ Please send a free catalog.

BRANDISH

DOUGLAS HIRT

FIRST TIME IN PAPERBACK!

Captain Ethan Brandish has finally given up his command of Fort Lowell, deep in Apache territory. But the vicious Apache leader, Yellow Shirt, has another fate in store for him. He and a group of renegade warriors attack a stage station and ride off just before Brandish arrives. But the Apaches are still out there—watching and waiting—and Brandish must risk his own life to save the few wounded survivors.

___4323-8 $4.50 US/$5.50 CAN

Dorchester Publishing Co., Inc.
P.O. Box 6640
Wayne, PA 19087-8640

Please add $1.75 for shipping and handling for the first book and $.50 for each book thereafter. NY, NYC, and PA residents, please add appropriate sales tax. No cash, stamps, or C.O.D.s. All orders shipped within 6 weeks via postal service book rate. Canadian orders require $2.00 extra postage and must be paid in U.S. dollars through a U.S. banking facility.

Name_____
Address_____
City_____State_____Zip_____
I have enclosed $_____ in payment for the checked book(s).
Payment <u>must</u> accompany all orders. ☐ Please send a free catalog.

DARK TRAIL

Hiram King

When the War Between the States was finally over, many men returned from battle only to find their homes destroyed and their families scattered to the wind. Bodie Johnson is one of those men. But while some families fled before advancing armies, the Johnson family was packed up like cattle and shipped west—on a slave train. With only that information to go on, Bodie sets out to find whatever remains of his family. And he will do it. Because no matter how vast the West is, no matter what stands in his way, Bodie knows one thing—the Johnsons will survive.

___4418-8 $5.50 US/$6.50 CAN

Dorchester Publishing Co., Inc.
P.O. Box 6640
Wayne, PA 19087-8640

Please add $1.75 for shipping and handling for the first book and $.50 for each book thereafter. NY, NYC, and PA residents, please add appropriate sales tax. No cash, stamps, or C.O.D.s. All orders shipped within 6 weeks via postal service book rate. Canadian orders require $2.00 extra postage and must be paid in U.S. dollars through a U.S. banking facility.

Name_____
Address_____
City_____ State_____ Zip_____
I have enclosed $_____ in payment for the checked book(s).
Payment <u>must</u> accompany all orders. ☐ Please send a free catalog.
      CHECK OUT OUR WEBSITE! www.dorchesterpub.com